STAY WITH ME, LELLA

Prose Series 54

MARISA LABOZZETTA

STAY WITH ME, LELLA

A NOVEL

GUERNICA
TORONTO·BUFFALO·LANCASTER (U.K.)
1999

Printed in Canada.
Typeset by Selina, Toronto.

Antonio D'Alfonso, Editor.
Guernica Editions Inc.
P.O. Box 117, Station P, Toronto (ON), Canada M5S 2S6
2250 Military Road, Tonawanda, N.Y. 14150-6000 U.S.A.
Gazelle, Falcon House, Queen Square, Lancaster LA1 1RN U.K.

Legal Deposit — First Quarter
National Library of Canada
Library of Congress Catalog Card Number: 98-75280
Canadian Cataloguing in Publication Data
Labozzetta, Marisa
Stay with me, Lella
(Prose series ; 32)
ISBN 1-55071-076-1
I. Title. II. Series.
PS3562.A2356S73   1999   813'.54   C98-901208-5

For my parents,
Viola and Michael Labozzetta,
with love and gratitude

But I was so much older then
I'm younger than that now.

Bob Dylan

I

THE DIGIACOMOS

In the country, Lella slept next to Johnny and Carla's room, in what was actually a small vestibule separated from the couple by nothing more than a closed door.

On the last night of their stay, Lella noticed that Carla, who always undressed in the bathroom, had gone fully clothed into the bedroom with Johnny. Lella pictured Carla, her head probably swimming in the lanquid aftermath of several highballs, disrobing in front of her husband. When the springs of the old mattress squeaked long beyond the time it took someone to settle into bed, Lella lifted herself from the pillow to hear better what was happening in the other room. The moaning began, and she wrapped her pillow around her head in an effort to block out the sounds.

That night Lella dreamed twice. In one dream, Lella was part of an audience of men and women who reverently filed by the still body of a naked woman lying on a table and touched whatever part of her they so desired.

In the second dream, it was Lella who lay naked on the table.

Johnny had been the first to arrive at the farm in a car packed with enough belongings to last more than their week's stay. His son Frankie, almost eleven, sat up front with his father, relegating his mother Carla to the back seat with his twelve-year-old sister Dolores and Lella — babysitter, housekeeper, cousin. (Lella's lack of title only manifested the ambiguity of her position within the family.)

"Frankie, change the station," Dolores ordered.

Johnny turned the dial quickly until the repetitious rock and roll beat slurred into the dreamy sound of orchestral strings.

"There! Leave it there! This — this is nice. Mantovani." Carla lit a cigarette and settled back into her seat.

"Momm, it's 1961, not 1950," Dolores moaned.

"Did we close the windows? Lella interrupted purposely. She sat between Carla and Dolores, her feet high on the hump in the center of the car's floor.

"Yes," Johnny said.

"The one in the bathroom?"

"Yes."

"I don't think I turned off the gas jets."

"You did," Carla assured her.

"We forgot to unplug the television."

"I did." Johnny held up an open hand and reached towards the back. Carla handed him her pack of Camels.

"Light one for me too," she said.

Johnny mumbled, trying to light two cigarettes he held between his lips with the lighter he had pulled out of the dashboard.

"Can you open the window a little?" Lella asked Carla.

"I'd rather not sit in a draft. I feel a cold coming on."

"A draft? For God's sake, Mom, it's boilin' out!"

"Open your window, will you?" Lella turned to Dolores.

"It'll mess my hair."

"Who cares about your stupid hair anyway. It looks like a rat's nest." Frankie burst into laughter.

"The smoke is making me nauseous. Open the window a crack, will you?" Lella insisted. Dolores pursed her lips.

"At home the smoke doesn't bother you. Here it bothers you," Carla said.

"Will you open the window, Dolores? I don't want her to get sick! Because if she gets sick, *I'll* get sick!" Frankie shouted.

"*Uffà!* Stop complaining, all of you!" Johnny put his cigarette out. "Open the window, Dolores."

Carla took her time finishing the Camel. She didn't light another one for the rest of the trip.

Soon it was the bumpiness of the road that led to the farm that got to them all. Johnny shifted into low gear and started up the hilly, rocky way. High weeds ran down its center and brushed the engine of the new white Impala as it pulled itself up the steep incline. The car had a turquoise interior with a thick matching stripe painted across the body. Lella and Dolores had wanted a red interior and stripe; Carla liked turquoise.

They called the place Paradise — nine acres of fields sealed away from neighbors by tall pines at the perimeters. Each year, when Johnny's parents, Aldo and Regina

DiGiacomo, first came up to spend the summer, the place looked more like a jungle. Weekend after weekend Aldo's three sons drove up to mow, clip, paint, and sculpture the landscape until it resembled the Garden of Eden. Far removed from the Brooklyn heat and grime, this *was* a paradise.

It was late August and the tomatoes were ready. Behind the white stucco house that Aldo and his sons had converted from a barn, smoke poured out of the old cook stove chimney.

Frankie left Lella's side and ran to his grandfather who stood next to a cauldron of boiling water used to sterilize mason jars. Frankie was as tall as Aldo, whose pants were held up with a belt forced into the tightest notch his barrel shape would permit. Aldo's ruddy complexion was clean-shaven, although he probably hadn't bathed for several days. He didn't like his wife Regina's sneaking his clothes into the wash too often either; he swore that the laundering would wear his outfits out quickly and, somehow, hasten his own mortality.

"Come, toin the handle." Aldo spoke English with the combination of a German and Brooklyn accent, the result of having first left his life as a shepherd in the hills not far from Rome when he was a teenager and gone to work in the steel mills of Eden, Germany. Lella had heard the story many times. Aldo returned to his Umbrian homeland only once, just long enough to marry Regina and father two sons. But he soon chose to live in America, leaving behind his brother, sister, and an ailing mother. Though he would send them money throughout the years, money to pay for their passage to New York, his mother never saw it. His brother had squandered it all.

When news of Aldo's mother's death reached more than a decade after his departure, Aldo cursed his brother in front of his own children, and cried like a baby.

Frankie grasped the handle of the machine that resembled a large meat grinder which chewed the seeds and skins of the tomatoes that Aldo had grown all summer. The pulpy red juice streamed down a slide at the opposite end and collected in a blackened vat. Regina poured the pureed mixture into the jars, added a basil leaf, and stored the mason jars away in the basement. During the occasional winter weekend visits she would bring back a fresh supply of jars and distribute them to the family back in Bensonhurst.

"You come too late. We need a'you to pick the tomatoes," Regina said to Carla who stood beside Lella. Regina was equal to her husband in stature; she was dark and emaciated-looking with a lusterless skin and wiry gray hair. Lella noticed that she was wearing, for the first time, the printed housedress Lella had given her for Christmas. As usual, her nylons were rolled down around her ankles above her black orthopedic shoes with holes at the heels for her spurs.

Regina did not hide the fact that she had not welcomed Carla into the DiGiacomo family. Whenever Carla said *geesta* instead of *questa* and *aoondi* instead of *dove*, Regina whispered to Lella, "She's Sicilian." In other words, what would one expect? Lella understood that, to Regina, Carla was a reminder of the impoverished southern extension of the old country that gave birth to mobsters. Carla had hailed from a people noted for their mystery and secrecy, and worst of all, who ate their pasta *after* their main dish instead of *before*. Carla did not help matters: she kept her spirit detached from the DiGiacomos, from most people. Just like her native Sicily, Carla was an island.

"Hello, Zia," Lella said. She bent down to kiss her Aunt Regina on the cheek, after Carla had failed to do so.

"*Bella,*" Regina said, beaming. The glossy white's of her eyes were thick-looking and yellowed like aged olive oil. As though Lella's head were an enormous prize tomato Regina had grown and was eager to pick, the old woman's bony hands reached up. Lella felt the calloused fingers spread over her skin, and claim, as Regina's own, Lella's smooth, round, unblemished face.

2

LELLA

Lella first came to live with Carla and Johnny when Dolores was sixteen months old. Lella had thick auburn hair, shiny round cheeks, pink lipstick, and full breasts and fanny. Lella sang, Lella shouted, Lella met Dolores at school with an umbrella on rainy days, dried her wet feet and covered them up with clean socks Lella had warmed on the radiator. It was Lella who rubbed Dolores's chest with Vicks Vapo Rub and then covered it with a hot cloth. It was Lella who fed her Junkett Rennet Custard by the spoonsful. It was Lella who tightened the scarf around Dolores's neck before she went out into the snow, Lella who sneaked Dolores a dime for ice cream from the Good Humor truck before dinner. And it was Lella who lay alongside her in the twin bed when she couldn't sleep, hugging her until Dolores's face was lost in the warmth and safety of the young woman's body.

Lella was the adopted daughter of a childless Calabrese couple, Angelina and Patsy Maglio. Whispers and rumors shaded the story of her natural parents who, she was told, had been Aldo's cousins. They had died of some infectious disease in the DiGiacomo Umbrian *paese* of Portaria when Lella was only two. Upon hearing the news, Aldo DiGiacomo supposedly paid the child's passage to New York and brought her to live with the Maglios who resided above their Italian specialty market on Eighteenth Avenue.

The commercial stretch of bland, flat roofed, and unadorned square brick architecture blended poorly with the new world. Garish red signs printed in bold gold letters announced the presence of pastry shops, grocers, pharmacists, and dentist. Their musical sounding names contrasted with those of the Jewish delicatessens and dry goods stores.

Angelina and Patsy Maglio never took vacations. They never left the *salumeria* where mozzarella balls were larger than grapefruits. Instead, every summer they permitted Lella to spend a month with the DiGiacomos at a boarding house on a dairy farm outside of the city. It was the acreage behind that farm that Regina and Aldo DiGiacomo later purchased from its owner who returned to Italy.

At an early age, Lella tied ribbons in her pigtails and rubbed berry juice on her lips. Twelve years her senior, Johnny taught her how to pitch a softball. He carried Lella on his shoulders through high weeds and entangling roots all the way to the lake so that she might keep up with him and his brothers. Her efforts to attract her cousin Johnny in the manner she had hoped, however, went unnoticed.

At night Lella prayed that Johnny would wait for her. She dreamed Johnny would fall in love with her and wondered how he had failed to notice her in that way before. And when Johnny's lips were about to touch hers, Lella would awaken.

The war broke out. Johnny was sent to the Pacific. Lella followed Johnny from new Guinea to the Philippines to Japan by writing him letters to which he faithfully replied. He called her pet names like *angel* and *kitten*. She dreamed that, one day, peace would be declared, and that she would meet his ship at the port and, marvelling how she had become a gorgeous irresistible young woman, Johnny would sweep her off her feet and into his arms, and tell her how he could not have survived without all of her letters. Again, just as he was about to plant the kiss, Lella would wake up.

But Lella did not meet Johnny at the port when the war ended. Nobody did. No one knew the exact date of Johnny's arrival. So he just showed up at the DiGiacomo door, unannounced, one hot afternoon in the summer of 1945. When Lella heard the news, she ran over to the house. Johnny did, in fact, take her up into his arms, and tell her how much she had changed. He thanked her for the beautiful letters, and, yes, Johnny kissed Lella on the lips. But it was not the kiss Lella had anticipated all those years. It was the same kiss Johnny had given to his mother, his sister Rose, and even Gerty Schwartz, the old woman next door.

Within weeks, Johnny met Carla, and six months later he married her. Johnny was twenty-two; Carla was twenty; Lella was ten.

Every day after school, Lella worked in her adopted parents' *salumeria* from the time she was able to scoop out a ball of mozzarella from a tub of water and weigh it without letting it role off the scale and onto the wooden floor. Just after her fifteenth birthday, a fire broke out in the market while the family slept above. The three had already fled to safety down the iron fire escape at the back of the building, when Lella's adopted mother Angelina insisted she and her husband Patsy go into the basement to salvage a new shipment of prosciutto. The exit became blocked, and the two of them, dead from smoke inhalation, were found huddled against one another and the stack of imported Italian ham.

This misfortune happened just at the time Carla became pregnant with Frankie and was mourning the fact that, with a toddler and an infant, she would never be able to go back to work. She hated dusting under beds and ironing Johnny's white boxer shorts and t-shirts. She was not much of a cook (although she did turn out superb rice balls).

She despised waiting for Johnny to wake up in the morning, get out of the bathroom, leave for work, then return home again. While the postwar boom of motherhood suited most women Carla's age, for Carla, parenting was a disillusionment. She did not enjoy preparing formula, shaking out diapers into the toilet, playing nonsensical games with Dolores on the linoleum kitchen floor and, above all, waiting for her daughter to take a nap so she could read Shakespeare, Gardner, anyone. She was bored, frustrated, and tired of her life hinging on everyone else's moves. Carla was a woman who relished her independence. She needed to earn her own money.

It was Carla's mother-in-law Regina who, fearing for the well-being of her son and grandchildren, suggested that Lella, now a teenage orphan, live with and help out Carla and Johnny.

And so Lella moved from the busy avenue to one of its side streets and the two-story apartment house that Johnny and Carla owned.

The entrance to the brick building led to a small foyer where the mailboxes hung side by side on a wall; a second door opened into a larger dark hallway. To the right was the apartment occupied by the tenants — a nosy mathematics teacher, who, out of respect, all the old Italians on the block called the Professor, and his newly arrived wife who, every Sunday morning, sang Italian opera in the shower. Straight ahead were the long flight of stairs that the DiGiacomos climbed daily to reach their apartment.

It was a railroad apartment, one room emptying into another, except for the front bedrooms which faced the street and which sat side by side — Carla and Johnny's to the right, Frankie's to the left. These bedrooms opened into the living room, followed by the dining room, a small foyer and bath, the kitchen, and finally, the room that Lella shared with Dolores.

The apartment house was attached to one just like it, then separated from another pair by a narrow alley where wash hung out on lines extending from kitchen windows to telephone poles. The series of flat-roofed buildings and alleyways continued along most of the block, the facades varying little. The only distinguishing feature of the DiGiacomo's apartment house was a pair of stately white stone lions that sat like sentinels on either side of the steps. A tall six-story apartment building stood like a mighty overseer in the center of the block, and a small row of brownstones with their chocolate-colored sandstone Renaissance fronts, long flights of steps, and double glass doors — reminders of an era long gone.

Lella was as much of a misfit to the family as was the six-story apartment house to the block's skyline. She engaged herself in the children's games as though she were searching for some lost chunk of her childhood that she refused to abandon or, perhaps, had never experienced. In contrast, she hid *True Confession* under her pillow and read it late at night after Dolores had fallen asleep. She would take the part of the characters in the stories, their romantic involvements becoming her own, and caress her body in an attempt to find pleasure evoked by some imaginary lover.

At first, Lella was expected to care for Dolores and Frankie and to perform light housework. But, as soon as Lella graduated from high school, Carla began a new job as a legal secretary for a posh firm on Madison Avenue which left Lella in complete charge of the household and children. Lella felt subordinate to Carla who went to business in spiked heels, blotted her lipstick with a piece of toilet tissue, and shared her bed with a man.

While berry juice had given way to makeup and pigtails to pin curls, Lella could not capture Johnny DiGiacomo's attention. Johnny affectionately regarded her as he did his younger sister Rose — genderless. That she worked for him did not alter the picture; in their culture, women were accustomed to catering to the men in their families.

Now and then, Lella would be slipped a few extra dollars for spending money without Carla's knowing. And she would be teased by Johnny about fictitious boyfriends, as though she were still a little girl. But, after taking a shower, she often emerged from the bathroom with her chenille robe dangling at her sides, revealing a woman's silhouette beneath a transparent nightgown. When, on Manhattan Beach, she offered Johnny a pepper and egg sandwich, she bent over him, forcing him to look at her large breasts or into her light brown eyes flecked with apple green, honest and hungry. Lella refused to believe these eyes might be pursuing his for something more than simple flirtation, something with enormous consequences, something she knew Johnny could not give.

3

CARLA

Carla DiGiacomo appeared to be the steady kind.

She had the awful habit of licking a perfumed handkerchief she found crumpled up at the bottom of her pocketbook and rubbing furiously at smudges on her children's faces.

She grabbed the toilet stall door from exiting women in subway restrooms before the door locked shut, so she did not have to deposit a dime.

Lella knew that every morning Carla tucked a five dollar bill and a subway token down her brassiere, in case she should be robbed or lose her purse. That way she could still get a cream cheese on date nut bread sandwich and a cup of coffee at Chock Full O' Nuts and catch the Sea Beach Express home.

She insisted Lella cut up cardboard cans of scouring powder to get at the remaining grains and turn ketchup bottles upside down to salvage the last slow-running drops before the bottle was discarded. But to Lella, Carla DiGiacomo was a bundle of contradictions, a philosophically inconsistent woman wedged between two worlds.

Carla was an avid reader who accepted as gospel anything in print; yet she thought Doctor Spock's theory of permissiveness was full of shit. While she could complete the *New York Times* crossword puzzle before Johnny located the sports section, she said that boys should be smarter than girls but that girls should be better looking. She kept black strap molasses, wheat germ, and yogurt in the refrigerator. She refused to make her Sunday gravy without rolled pig's skin. She insisted her husband and children eat at least one egg a day.

She told Frankie and Dolores that with education they could accomplish anything in life. She urged them to exercise moderation in their choice of activities and hope for the best.

She never got too happy or too depressed. She believed that it wasn't ladylike to say one had to go to the bathroom: so she excused herself by explaining she had a *call*.

She smoked two packs of Camels a day.

She told Lella that it was a woman's obligation in life to multiply and make a man's home as comfortable as possible. Yet Carla never stayed home with her own children. Johnny's frequent innuendo directed at Carla led Lella to believe that Carla also did not submit herself sexually whenever it pleased her husband.

Carla liked to tell her story to Lella and the children, every detail of it: she had been born in Philadelphia a month after her parents arrived from Sicily. When she was fifteen, her parents moved to Brooklyn where her father went into business with his cousin. They would not only repair shoes, but make them as well. Her father gave his trade its full glory. It was in the shoe repair shop that

Carla first encountered a DiGiacomo — not Johnny but his older brother Louie.

Carla had stopped in one day after school to bring her father his lunch. Louie DiGiacomo was picking up a pair of shoes Carla's father had just put new heels on. Louie was apparently quite taken with Carla's classic beauty — dark hair and eyes, strong but straight nose, velvety skin, and immediately tried to get her attention. Carla ignored him and walked out of the store.

"Pardon me," he said." Could I invite you for a cup of coffee?"

"Why?" Carla eyed him distrustfully.

"You live in the neighborhood?"

"I'm on my way to the library."

"I see. I'll walk with you. I like libraries."

"Really?" She perked up.

"Yeah. You know. Quiet. No noise. Yeah, I like them. All those books that people actually wrote. It's fascinatin'. So where do you go to school?"

"New Utrecht."

"You look older than a high school girl."

"Are you at City College?" she asked.

"Me?"

Louie had never stepped foot in a college. In fact, Louie dropped out of high school after his sophomore year. At the time he was taking a two-week evening course given by The Gummy World Company on how to push twice as much penny candy in half the sales pitch time.

Carla could tell Louie sensed he was getting into something above his head. "I just realized I have an appointment all the way downtown. Maybe we can grab that coffee another time. It's been a pleasure talkin' with you," Louie said and ran off without even having asked her name.

When they met years later, neither Louie nor Carla ever acknowledged that the encounter had taken place.

By the time Carla graduated from high school, her father's business had soured: people preferred to buy their shoes ready-made from Thom McAn. Besides, her father's partner had spent the profits at the race track. Carla was expected to decline her acceptance to a free education at Hunter College and get a job. Bound by her parents' narrow old-world outlook and her own sense of duty, Carla felt doomed. She worked as a receptionist in a law firm, taking free shorthand and business courses at night school. If she could not go to college, she would at least become the best secretary around. The year Carla and Johnny had Dolores, her mother died of a massive stroke and, within a month, her father passed away broken hearted.

Carla never hid the fact that Dolores did not turn out to be anything like Carla had expected. Johnny was fair-skinned with blond hair, light blue eyes, and an aquiline nose, just like Aldo's. Carla said that when Dolores was conceived, Carla assumed that her genes and Johnny's would mesh in perfect combination; she anticipated a child with her own raven hair and chiseled features and her husband's fair skin and azure eyes. But the girl's complexion was rather sallow, not dark and mellow like Carla's, and certainly not rosy like Johnny's. Her hair and eyes were light brown which offered no contrast to her skin coloring. She did possess Johnny's long nose with its characteristic bump — handsome on a man, Carla acknowledged, but detrimental to a woman's looks. Carla did not hide her disappointment: it was as though she had mixed black and white, hoping for polka dots; instead, she got gray. She called her Dolores — a name that meant pain and sorrow.

Frankie, on the other hand, had Carla's face. After he was born, Regina said Carla had just spit and Frankie appeared, so strong was the similarity.

☆

On her tenth birthday, Dolores expressed her first and last interest in cooking. Out of nowhere she stated that, as soon as she became a teenager, she would leave home and live on her own.

Dolores sat on the red kitchen stepstool and watched Lella cut off the tips of an eggplant and rub the pieces against the raw ends of the eggplant.

"What are you doing that for?" Dolores asked.

"It takes the bitterness away."

"Who said?"

"My mother. She always did this."

"Your real mother or your adopted mother?"

Although Angelina Maglio had died before Dolores was even born, Carla made sure to let her children know that Lella had been adopted. Carla believed in the truth.

"My adopted mother," Lella answered.

"Who told your mother?" Dolores asked.

"God! I don't know, Dolores. I guess her mother."

"Your adopted mother's mother," Dolores confirmed.

"Yes."

Lella sliced the rest of the eggplant, salted it, and piled it high in a bowl. Dolores covered the mound with an inverted saucer and placed an electric iron, the long cord wrapped around its handle, for weight.

"Bernadette Scoma already wears a bra but I don't have anything," Dolores said, staring down at her flat chest.

"You will one day," Lella assured her.

"How do you know? My mother isn't very busty. I wish *you* were my mother."

Lella smiled. She often felt as though she was Dolores and Frankie's mother. She sometimes imagined it so.

"What's that stuff?" Dolores observed the black liquid secreted by the eggplant and which was collecting in the bottom of the bowl.

"Poison."

Dolores was grating a large ball of mozzarella when Carla entered. "Come with me." Carla motioned with her finger. She stared straight at Dolores and ignored Lella.

"But I'm cooking with Lella."

"This will just take a few minutes."

Carla handed her daughter a thin pamphlet. It was frayed along the edges and some of the corners of pages were missing. It was the same book Lella's mother had given to her when she was eleven, and God only knew to whom else it had been passed around to before and after her. Dolores, holding on tightly to *Now You Are Ten: An Introduction to Womanhood,* followed her mother into the parlor. From the kitchen and across the tiny foyer,

Lella could see the mother and daughter sit down on the couch together.

Carla picked up her pack of cigarettes from the end table and went into her bedroom. Lella watched as Dolores turned the pages quickly. "Menstruation," she stumbled on the pronunciation. A few minutes later, Carla was back.

"Did you understand it, Dolores?" Carla sat down next to her.

"Yeah."

"You know what it means?"

"What?"

"You can have a baby. That is once you get your period, you're a woman."

Lella shook her head.

"How do you get it?" Dolores looked at her with uncertainty.

"Maybe this year. Maybe next. I was eleven, but I was precocious. I developed early on and . . ."

"But *how* will I get it?"

"It just happens to you. You'll see it. You bleed." She lowered her voice, although no one else but Lella was home. "Down below. That's where everything happens."

"It's like going to the bathroom?"

Lella laughed out loud, then pretended to be coughing.

"Not exactly. You know, my mother never said a word about sex, and when I got my *friend* or the curse, as we used to call it, I thought I was dying. That's what sanitary napkins are for, you know."

"Sex?"

"Your friend, Dolores. Your period," she mumbled. "Don't be ashamed when you have to buy them in the drugstore. Everyone knows what you need them for. Besides, they always wrap the box in brown paper, so no one else will see it. You know, when I was a girl, we had to use rags."

"Ugh!"

"When it happens," Carla continued. "Just tell me."

"Or Lella," Dolores interrupted.

Carla ignored her.

"And if it happens in school, tell Sister. She'll know what to do. She's a woman too, you know," Carla said.

"Underneath all those black robes?"

"Yes, there's a real woman."

"With all the parts?"

"Yes, Dolores," Carla became annoyed.

Lella had felt it coming. It never took long for Dolores to irritate Carla. It was a simple yet common progression of what, according to Carla, were naive questions that Dolores insisted on asking. Before very long, she would ask one question too many.

"Good," Carla said, standing up, happy to have it over with, and pleased with her candidness. "Oh, and Dolores, they say plants die when you touch them, so don't go into Grandpa's garden when you have it. He gets very upset if he knows."

"Do they?"

"What?"

"Die."

"I really don't know. I never touch a plant when I have it." Carla walked over to her daughter and swept the long bangs out of her daughter's eyes with her hand. "Show your forehead, honey; it's a sign of intelligence."

Dolores remained on the turquoise sectional, staring at the sandalwood and brown print fiberglass drapes.

So, Lella thought, Dolores has had her first crash course in sex. Soon she would be a woman.

"Now I know," Dolores told Lella.

"Know what?"

"The notes — and the other thing. I know," she said proudly.

Several times a day in class, Bernadette Scoma (who lived next door to the DiGiacomos in old lady Yahtzbin's apartment house) giggling, would hand Dolores a small rectangular piece of memo pad paper upon which she had printed in huge letters, *period*. Not having the slightest notion of what she was referring to, Dolores had accepted the note and returned the giggle. Occasionally during recess, while standing in line to take their turns jumping rope, Bernadette would turn around to Dolores, cup her hand over her mouth whisper "period," and giggle.

After Carla's lecture, Dolores ran to the dictionary that her mother kept in the bathroom where, after dinner, Carla did her crossword puzzles.

Lella knocked at the bathroom door and opened it a crack.

"Hurry up, Dolores. I have to go," Lella said.

"In a minute."

Dolores turned to the M's. Her disappointment was paralleled to that of having once looked up *prophylactic* after finding a box of Trojans in her father's dresser drawer.

menstruation. n. Physiol. 1. The periodical flow of bloody fluid from the uterus, occurring normally about every 28 days; also called catamenia, menses. 2. An occurrence of this flow; also called period.

"Dolores," Lella called again.

"I'm constipated."

Dolores flipped a few pages ahead to *prophylactic* as though the meaning might somehow have changed, become clearer to her.

prophylactic. adj. Tending to prevent or ward off something, especially disease; preventive. n. A prophylactic medicine or appliance.

Walking home from school one day, there had been a prophylactic fully opened, lying in the gutter. Dolores thought it was a finger of a large-sized rubber glove, but Bernadette Scoma told her it was a scumbag. "You know, rubber, Trojan, for the F-word," she had said. Dolores didn't know. She ran home and asked Lella what a scumbag was.

"What men wear during sex," a flustered Lella had answered. Little did Lella know how much she had confused Dolores who, today, saw everything as becoming clearer to her. Dolores emerged from the bathroom and smiled smugly at Lella who stood waiting, unaware of jumble of newly discovered knowledge Dolores carried with her:

Men also got their period, but they used prohylactics instead of sanitary napkins. Having your friend was fucking — sex. And to do it, you needed sanitary napkins and Trojans. Up until that day, for Dolores, *fuck* had only been a dirty word eighth graders at Blessed Trinity spray-painted at night in the schoolyard, but were forbidden to say.

4

LELLA AND ROSARIO

Lella never returned to Bensonhurst with Johnny and Carla when their week at the farm was over that summer. Rosario had come to visit one afternoon.

Aldo squeeled with delight at the sight of Rosario in the state trooper's car, with its flashing red beacon and wailing siren, making its way up the road. Carla went into the bathroom to touch up her lipstick.

Rosario's family, local dairy farmers, was a novelty: they had immigrated after the war, bringing with them tales of a fascist Italy inconceivable to the DiGiacomos, who first met Rosario when he was fifteen and unable to speak English. Now, every autumn, he brought pounds of venison, a souvenir of a deer that had been illegally shot by some hunter and taken away by Rosario. Butchered and neatly packaged in freezer wrap, it was an offering made to Aldo out of respect for his parents' friendship and in the hopes that it would bring him closer to Lella.

When the *bocce* game was over and coffee and cake had been served, Rosario led Frankie over to his car. He let Frankie examine the radio and turn on the flashing light.

Lella and Carla carried cups and saucers back into the house. Carla lit a cigarette. Lella filled a small basin with water.

"Mamma's so worried about conserving the water in that well . . . Aren't you just dying to get home and open all the faucets just for·the hell of it?" Carla laughed. Her deep, raspy chuckle turned into a loose cough.

"Why don't you go out for some air?" Lella said.

"And why are you washing those dishes over again? You just did them."

"The water's so hard here. Nothing seems to get clean."

"You know, you're crazy. I'm going to steel another one of these." Carla pointed to an empty pack of Camels and walked out just as Rosario was coming in.

Rosario was tall, much taller than the DiGiacomo men, and darker. His body was muscular, the tendons in his arms becoming prominent any time he lifted a lawn chair or grasped the slight DiGiacomo men in a hand-shake. He wore a pale blue sports shirt and the khaki trousers of his uniform. At thirty years old, his English was perfect-*charming*, the DiGiacomo women said, with just the right trace of an Italian accent.

"I'd like to take you to a movie tonight. I know you like movies," he said.

"Oh, I can't. We're leaving this evening."

Lella continued scrubbing the glass she held in her hand. Rosario made her nervous. She had only dated one other man, Vinnie the butcher, a few times but was never attracted to him. Rosario's body stirred up something within her, although the intensity of his gaze and the seriousness in his voice irked her.

"Couldn't you stay here with *compare* Aldo and *comare* Regina a few more days."

"I have to take care of the children back home."

"We can manage," Johnny broke in, as he emerged from the bathroom, one hand holding the *Daily News*, the other checking his fly.

"But how will I get back?" Lella asked Johnny, surprised at the ease with which he offered to give her up.

"I'll come up and get you next Saturday."

"That's a whole week."

"Don't worry. Frankie and Dolores will be fine." He suggested that Louie's wife Adrienne could help look after them. "The kids are getting big, you know," he said as he picked a piece of lint off of his pant leg.

Later, as Lella watched Johnny's Impala wobbling slowly back down the bumpy road, kicking up stones and dust, she was sure she had made a mistake. Frankie sat on his knees, facing the rear window, and waved madly at her until he and the car became nothing more than a speck she could no longer hold on to. Lella stayed on the road for awhile, hoping they would reappear and claim her. They never did.

The closest movie theater to the farm was outdoors, about a ten-minute ride along the unlit winding Raspberry Lane. As Rosario drove beyond the speed limit, the red light flashing above, Lella braked with her foot and held on tightly to the doorknob, as though ready to eject at any moment. Her eyes fixed on the statue of Saint

Christopher sitting on the dashboard: if he got her to and from the theater in one piece, she would never complain about anything again.

"Do you like it?" Rosario asked Lella, referring to the three and one half hour *Exodus*. His fingers made circles on her skin; his palm remained firmly planted on the bare shoulder that her halter dress exposed. His touch alerted the nerve-endings in her nipples and created a tightening down in her groin. If only it weren't Rosario, Lella kept telling herself, sitting like a piece of carved marble alongside him.

He bought her a shrimp roll and cup of coffee during the intermission. The moment the second part began, Rosario smothered Lella's mouth with his. Large, it sealed itself to the areas above and below her mouth with warm saliva. Lella kissed him back, sucking hard, the two of them creating a vacuum. His hand crept down and rested on her breast. She liked the feeling. She also liked the sensation of his knee, nuzzling into her crotch. She wanted him to press harder there, end the gnawing, but instead of moving closer to him, she became full of guilt and pushed him away. He was breathing heavily, beads of perspiration from his face had dripped onto hers. He let go of her and rested his elbows on the steering wheel, holding his head in his hands in an effort to compose himself.

"Sorry," he said.

"I'd like to go."

"It's just been such a long time since I've been with anyone like you."

Lella didn't answer him. She had wanted him to do things to her and that must have been wrong, especially when she didn't even really like *him*, just his body. Still she was worried about what he was thinking of her for having let him go so far. Carla would certainly laugh at Lella. "What a fool you are," she would say.

Rosario started up the engine. With the palm of his hand he wiped the fogged up windshield, leaving the glass blurry and streaky. As he pulled out of his parking spot, glass crashed and there was a loud bang. Rosario slammed on the breaks; Lella banged her head against the CB radio.

Rosario had forgotten to remove the movie speaker from the window. They didn't speak until he walked her to the house; he was too embarassed. That's what made him so unappealing to her — his dullness, his lack of humor. At the door, he asked if he might phone her later in the week. Lella said yes, although she knew that, when he did, she would never consent to go out with him.

In the kitchen, she sat up drinking a glass of lemonade at the old enamel-top table and listened to the sounds of sleep coming from Aldo and Regina's room. Aldo snored and kept rhythm to the noisy ticking of the alarm clock on his nightstand. Regina wheezed every now and then.

Lella missed Frankie. She could no longer bribe him to come shopping on the avenue with her by promising him a slice of pizza or offering him a movie. She missed seeing his dark head of hair against his white pillow. She was losing him.

"Stay with me, Lellie," Frankie used to say at bed-time when he was younger.

His big black eyes reminded her of olives floating in giant tubs at her parents' *salumeria*.

"Forever," he'd add.

Lella brushed the hair off of his forehead.

She wanted to keep him that size always — small, containable, bundled up in the drab green blanket that had *US Army* printed in bold black letters. A token of his father's war days. She would bend over him and kiss the smooth taut skin.

He'd stick his nose into her cushiony breasts and sniff.

"What are you doing?" She'd be amused.

"Smelling you . . . Mmm, good."

He'd wriggle like a snake beneath the covers and take off his top.

"I'm hot," he'd say, and hand her the pajama top. "Make me into dough," he'd plead.

"It's late," she always said.

Yet she'd pull down the covers and begin to rotate the little body back and forth like a rolling pin, telling him over and over again about the delicious bread he was about to become. With the side of her hand, she'd pretend to slice him into little buns and shove him into an imaginary oven. Frankie laughed hysterically. She attempted to eat him up, scooping him into her arms. They'd hug each other hard. His hands were large for a little boy's. Like a carpenter's, his father said. Like a pianist, his mother insisted. Lella would pull the covers over him and watch his long black lashes slowly sweep down over his eyes. She'd wait a few moments, tiptoe to the door, and shut the light.

"Turn it on!" Frankie always said, his eyes still closed. The room would brighten with the security of artificial daylight. Lella slowly shut the door again.

Later, she'd check on him. She usually found him hidden beneath a tangled mess of sheets and blankets, his face red, his hair soaked with perspiration. She'd make him comfortable for the night and kiss him one last time.

But Frankie was in Brooklyn, and she was here for six more days, stuck like the flies on the curly brown strips of paper that hung from the fluorescent light fixture above. The only consolation was the thought that Johnny would soon come to get her. She would have the entire two-hour drive (maybe longer if there was traffic) alone with him. Her thoughts turned to what it would have been like to have been at the drive-in theater with Johnny, having Johnny's mouth on her mouth, his hands on her breasts.

In three days Lella helped Aldo and Regina can one hundred and twenty-five jars of tomatoes and forty-two jars of peaches and pears. They shelled pecks of kidney beans, took the seeds from pumpkins and squash and left them to dry. They stored some to be planted next spring. Lella and Regina washed all the linens and carried them up the narrow attic stairs where they folded them into cartons. They rubbed salt into the scatter rugs to loosen the dirt. Then they hung the rugs over a clothesline and beat them with brooms until the all the dirt and salt was gone. Aldo took the rabbits and pigs to a neighbor to keep during the winter, and Lella scrubbed and waxed the kentile floors. They picked the last bunch of grapes.

Lella was such a help to the old couple, they were able to close up the house and leave several days earlier. Johnny was not coming for her.

☆

On Lella'a first night back, Johnny and Carla took the family to Lella's favorite Chinese restaurant on the avenue.

"He always thought he shit ice cream," Johnny said about Rosario, as the waiter cleared away their plates.

"I find him very attractive," Carla said.

"He's a screwball. You know he shot me once. That's why he became a trooper — to use guns. Two years in combat, and the only time I ever got wounded was by that moron."

"You let me go out with a moron?" Lella said.

"You like him."

"When did he shoot you, Dad?" Frankie was excited.

"We were kids. My little brother Tony came up the country with his first pair of glasses one summer and Rosario wouldn't stop teasing him. When I told Rosario to cut it out, he shot me with a BB gun. Nicked my ear lobe." Johnny pointed to the spot.

"What did Grandpa do?"

"You didn't tell your Grandpa too much in those days."

Johnny stirred a melting ball of vanilla ice cream around in its blue and white saucer. "To him, the stranger was always right."

"You'd believe me, wouldn't you, Dad?"

"You bet, Buddy."

"Oh, that was so long ago," Carla said.

"You know what my brother Louie always says: 'A leper never changes his spots.' Of course, he means leopard."

"You don't have to translate it," Dolores moaned.

At home Lella caught up with all the children's news, then she joined Johnny and Carla in the parlor. Johnny stared at the television screen with a blank expression. Carla smoked a cigarette and balanced a cup of coffee on her lap.

"Lella, sit down. We need to talk to you," Carla began. She picked a piece of tobacco from her tongue with her thumb and index finger.

Lella sat on the couch across from Johnny and Carla. Her fingers nervously played with the hem of her skirt.

"Don't worry. It's something good. Lella, it's time for you to be on your own," Carla said it.

"You want me to go?"

"Lella, we're not putting you out into the street. But we think if you were on your own, you'd have more of a chance to meet people, have your own place. You know *compare* Dominick, the lawyer in Manhattan? You could start out by working in his office. You took typing and shorthand. You could become a legal secretary like me!"

"You already spoke to him?" Lella was shocked.

"I called him yesterday," Johnny finally broke into the conversation. "He'll pay you much more than we do, and you'll be able to live upstairs from his sister. There's an vacant one-bedroom in her building. You'll be out everyday, dressing nicely, riding the subways into work. It'll be exciting."

"I don't dress nicely?"

"You do." Johnny eyed the halter dress she had worn on her date with Rosario. "But the children are getting big now and — "

"And you don't need me! You're throwing me out. You're my *comare*, Carla — my best friend!"

"We're not throwing you out," Carla said.

Lella, who had never answered them back before, could see she had surprised Carla by her response. This fired Lella up more.

"Yes, you are! You took the best years of my life — my child-bearing years, used me like a dish rag, and now you're finished."

"Oh for godsake, Lella." Carla lit another cigarette. "You're twenty-six years old!"

"You want me to go? I'll go."

"It's for your own good. We don't want you to wait until you really *are* old and used up. Go now, while you're still young enough to get married and have your own family. Go out with men. Have fun," Carla said.

Lella was silent.

Johnny shifted with discomfort. Lella was glad.

"Look! You can't stay here forever! We don't owe it to you. You're not even a relative," Carla said.

"What are you talking about? My mother was Uncle Aldo's cousin."

Johnny glared at Carla, warning her not to bring up Lella's past. "What I mean is you're *not* old. You're a young woman, but you'll be old before you know it like old lady Yahtzbin next door. All she has is that lousy apartment house and everyone hates her. Do you want everyone to hate you?"

"*Basta*, Carla! Don't get carried away," Johnny said.

"I'm in the way, so I'll go," Lella shouted. "I'll marry the first ass that looks my way — maybe Rosario — " She looked at Johnny. "And have ten kids, and he'll probably beat us, but you'll be happy. You'll have your house to yourselves and your children will be healthy and grown up because I raised them! I wiped their behinds while you were riding the subways, and I sat up with them when they were sick, and ironed your lousy underwear, and cleaned your toilet. I'll go now. But don't call me when you need someone to do your dirty work because *I'll* be living it up riding the subways!"

"Lower your voice, Lella. You know how the professor and his wife listen at their door," Carla admonished.

Lella ran to her room, wiping her tear-filled face with her hands.

"*Ma questa è una casa di pazzi!*" Johnny said, throwing up his hands in despair.

"If this is a crazy house, it's only because you two live in it," Carla yelled back.

"Look what you've done," Johnny said.

"Me? This was your idea too."

"It was a lousy idea. How many women do you know live alone? Italian ones," Johnny said.

"Then let her go live with your parents; they love her so much."

"Carla, this is her home. When a girl has no parents, where does she live? With a brother or a sister, right? Well, that's what we are to her, a brother and sister. How can we expect her to live alone?"

"She won't be alone. She'll be upstairs from *compare* Dominick's sister."

"And who the hell is she? Lella belongs here with us. What were we thinking?"

The phone rang. It was Regina. She couldn't get her new television to work in time for the late news.

"I'll be right over, Ma," Johnny said. He turned to Carla. "You take care of Lella, okay?"

"Oh sure. I had to start it, now I have to finish it. Why couldn't your mother have called your brothers Louie or Tony?"

"Because she called me!"

"Everybody calls you. The world's keeper."

"Watch yourself, Carla." Johnny pointed a finger at her.

"Don't threaten me."

Lella heard Johnny leave for his parents' house, and she waited for Carla to come in and make amends.

By midnight everyone was back in their beds: Lella relieved; Carla clinging desperately to the edge of her side of the mattress.

"I never thought she'd react like that. Never would have guessed she had it in her," Johnny said.

"You wouldn't," Carla said.

"You saying I'm stupid?"

"Just blind where she's concerned."

"You mad?" Johnny asked Carla as they lay back to back.

"Yeah."

"I knew you were mad."

"A genius."

"Pretend it never happened," he said.

"I'm not mad."

"You sure?"

"God damnit, Johnny. I'm not mad! So what I don't come first in your life? I don't even come second or third."

In the morning, Lella prepared breakfast as usual. Johnny ate his two sunnyside-up eggs and slice of toast; the children drank their eggnogs. Carla, however, took a long time to get dressed. When she came into the kitchen, she took her place at the table. Lella felt Carla's eyes on her as Lella flitted around Carla's kitchen. Lella turned to Carla and smiled:

"Good morning, *comare*."

5

EVERYONE CRIES

From the time Lella had begun to prepare for her First Holy Comunion at seven years old to her Confirmation at eleven, she, along with other Catholic children, was excused early from public school every Wednesday afternoon. From one p.m. to three p.m., she attended catechism classes at Blessed Trinity Parochial School.

Lella had spent over four years mentally undressing the numerous veiled figures who stood at the front of the classrooms and differed only in height and width. She had rearranged the black-headed straight pins, sashes, and tucks, certain that if one pin were removed, the right one, the entire habit would come undone, except, of course, for the headpiece which, Lella believed, was molded onto nuns the day they took their final vows and sawed off each time their heads were shaved. Or was their hair just cut short? No one knew for sure. The part that interested her most was the bodice. Most nuns were entirely flat with a series of vertical pleats running down their level chest. But then there were those who no matter how many corsets they fastened around their breasts, could not conceal the bulging cushion that extended from neck to waist. Sister Miriam Devine's exception to this rule had led to the joke: What's black white and concave? Sister Devine, of course.

One afternoon, Sister Devine had accused a busty eleven-year old Lella of being a brazen hussy who wore falsies.

"God is merciful," Sister Devine said. "You might still get to heaven if you go to confession and make the Stations of the Cross every day for the rest of your life."

Now it was Dolores, an eighth grade student at Blessed Trinity, who sat daily in front of Sister Devine. Short, dark, and wrinkled, were it not for the starched white bib that sprung from her neck and the white cast-like headdress that squeezed out two eyes, a nose, a mouth, and two fleshy hanging jowls, Sister Devine would have been four feet six inches of heavy black folds and a pair of giant black wooden rosary beads.

"Bring me your face," she demanded of the mischievous young men who automatically knelt. She aligned their profiles with her bony hand that then delivered a smack powerful enough to leave the imprint of her five fingers on their cheeks. Sister Devine combed the aisles after math exams, punching the boys and yanking the girls' hair for every wrong answer they had given. Dolores never told her parents; she got her hair cut.

Sister Devine called the boys' adolescent sexual inquisitiveness the work of the devil and sent them to the lavatory to wash every time she caught one with his hands in the most remote vicinity of his zipper. She once saw Frankie in the corridor with his fly open. "Button up!" she instructed him. He nervously checked his shirt. He figured he had misunderstood the nun when he found the buttons intact, so he began to unbutton them. The gesture merited a slap from Sister Devine who proceeded to staple the boy's tie to the bulletin board at the entrance of the school where he was to remain for an entire morning — a reminder to all of the consequences of deviant behavior.

Sister Devine told the girls that only harlots wore shorts and see-through blouses. Young girls who did got cut into pieces by lecherous men.

Carla and Johnny never heard these stories from Dolores and Frankie. Lella, however, was privy to the tales after school over cookies and milk.

Every day during recess, several students in Sister Devine's class were allowed to remain in the empty third-floor classroom to give remedial help to fellow classmates. Sister Devine took the rest of the children out to the schoolyard.

Dolores was helping Bernadette Scoma find the area of a circle one afternoon, when she felt extremely moist in the crotch.

"Come with me into the wardrobe," Dolores whispered to Bernadette. "I think I have it."

Two boys were diagramming sentences in the next row. Bernadette walked closely behind Dolores in case Dolores had stained her skirt.

"Is this your first time?" Bernadette closed the door to the long, narrow wardrobe.

"Yeah."

Dolores fumbled through her book satchel which hung on a hook and removed the sanitary napkin and two safety pins wrapped in a torn, linty, pink tissue she had been carrying around since Carla's talk about womanhood two years ago. With her back to Bernadette, Dolores picked up her skirt and offered it to Bernadette to hold, while Dolores pulled down her garter belt and proceeded to pin the napkin to her soiled panties.

"You got it on backwards," Bernadette said.

"Big deal." Dolores was sweating.

Out of nowhere, brilliant light flooded the dark closet. The girls turned towards it and shielded their eyes. Aghast, Sister Devine stood at the opened doorway. She ordered the two out. There were no explanations to be offered.

"Dirty girls," she snarled. "Dirty, dirty, perverted girls!"

After school, Dolores handed Lella the crisp white envelope that seemed to have been starched along with the bib of Sister Devine's habit. In faultless penmanship was written: *Mr. and Mrs. John DiGiacomo.*

"I can't open this," Lella protested.

"Please, Lellie. I need to know how bad it is."

Lella steamed the envelope open over a pot of boiling water, while Dolores told her story.

"Neat!" Frankie stood almost mesmerized as the envelope flap began to curl away from its seal.

February 3, 1962
Dear Mr. and Mrs. DiGiacomo:

It is my regret to inform you that your daughter Dolores has been found employing behavior inappropriate of the student body at Blessed Trinity. Therefore, I request that you remove her at once.

Mother Superior and I shall expect you tomorrow at 1:45 p.m. I continue to pray for Dolores.

A.M.D.G.

Sister Miriam Devine

"What does A.M.D.G. mean?" Lella asked.

"It's a Latin abbreviation: *All for the honor and glory of God*. You'll go and talk to her, won't you, Lellie?"

"I'm not your mother."

"Well, you kind of are. Please, Lellie. You can talk them out of it."

"I don't know, Dolores."

"Pleeeese. I'll keep our bedroom clean and help you fold the laundry for a year." Dolores began to cry.

"All right. I'll try."

"I'm tellin'," Frankie said, eyes wide open with disbelief.

"Frankie, Lella's like our mother, right? So it's okay. It'll just be our secret. I'll give you half of my allowance this week."

"All of it."

"All of it."

The next day, Lella put on her black straight skirt and the white blouse with a Peter Pan collar. She blotted her lipstick with a tissue, the way Carla did; put a kerchief over her head to protect her bouffant hairdo from the wind, the way Carla did; made sure the gas jets were turned off on the stove; and set out for Blessed Trinity. As she rode the bus up Sixtieth Street, she rehearsed over and over again the plea she would make for Dolores. After all, this was the child's first offense. Something like it would never happen again. In fact, it really hadn't happened. It was all just a mistake. Being women, surely they understood.

Lelia sat in the principal's office, the blinds closed, the radiators hissing. She fixated on a nearly life-sized statue of the Virgin Mary; she heard the chanting of the

Litany in a nearby classroom. Other than the recitation, the corridors were still, dark, and shiny. A class silently marched on tiptoe past the office. Lella strained to see if Frankie was in the group. While she looked, Sister Thomas Aquinas and Sister Devine entered, shutting the door behind them and obstructing Lella's view.

"I'm Sister Thomas Aquinas," the pale elderly nun with chalky lips said.

Lella thought she might have been embalmed ahead of time. Nuns were always boasting about being prepared for the afterlife.

"This is Sister Miriam Devine," Sister Aquinas added.

Sister Devine took a hard look at Lella, her eyebrows knitted up quizzically. Then she relaxed them and focused her gaze on Sister Aquinas.

"If you'll just sign the withdrawal form, Mrs. DiGiacomo, the matter will be settled as quickly and neatly as possible. By the way, it might comfort you to know that I have expelled Bernadette Scoma also," Sister Aquinas said.

"I thought we might talk about this, Sister. After all the girl had only gotten her — "

"Mrs. DiGiacomo, there is nothing to talk about. Are you disputing what Sister Devine walked in on?"

"Well, actually, Sister, I was going to try to explain to you what had really — "

"Mrs. DiGiacomo. My school is overflowing with enrollment. Sister Devine has forty-eight students in her classroom. Sister Celeste's first grade has sixty-four. We cannot tolerate any deviant conduct. We do not need your daughter. Have I made myself clear?" She handed the form and an uncovered fountain pen to Lella.

Lella hesitated.

"Mrs. DiGiacomo," Sister Aquinas prodded.

Lella took a deep breath and quickly signed Carla's name. On the way home, she stopped in a doorway next to a drug store and vomited in the vestibule. Carla and Johnny would surely throw her out now.

"They made me sign," she told Dolores when she arrived home.

"Good. I hate the place," Dolores said.

"I told you," Frankie said.

"I think the Good Humor man's out front." Lella handed Frankie a quarter for an ice cream.

"I told you," the boy shouted behind his back as the apartment door slammed shut.

"God! I can't believe I did that, Dolores. What am I going to do?" Lella said.

"Stop calling on God. He's on their side."

Johnny blamed it all on Bernadette Scoma whom he had always thought to be oversexed and, as he put it, not quite right in that area. His eyes welled up with tears and he cast his hands up to the heavens in distress.

"How could I have a daughter who could be persuaded by someone like that Bernadette? It's one thing to be a delinquent. That I could handle."

He raised his arm as though preparing to render a smack, then cast both hands up again. In actuality, Johnny never touched the children. When Frankie was brought home by the police for tapping the wire to the pay phone in Harold Berger's candy store, Johnny had taken a whole watermelon from the refrigerator, hurled it out the front window, and then had Frankie clean it up, rather than touch his son.

"You did this to her," Johnny told Carla. "You had to give her a name that meant pain and suffering. That's why she's mixed up like that."

"Stop behaving like a fool." Carla poured him a shot of Benedictine and Brandy. "There's nothing wrong with your daughter. It's those nuns. They're the perverted ones. And you know what? This whole thing's your fault, because public school wasn't good enough for your kids. They had to go to parochial school!"

"Dad, who do you believe? Me or them?" Dolores said.

Johnny was silent.

Crying, Dolores ran to the bathroom.

"I'll tell you where the problem is here. It's with you!" Carla pointed to Lella. "How could you pretend to be me? How could you dare?"

"I'm sorry. I don't know what I was thinking. I thought I'd save you the grief — but instead I just made it worse. I'm sorry," Lella said.

"You should be!"

"*Basta*, Carla," Johnny said.

"*Basta?* Now I should be quiet? Because *she's* involved? You didn't even believe your own daughter!"

"I believe her. I'm relieved."

"You give everyone *agita*. Then you're relieved."

Lella bit her lips to conceal her tears and ran to her room. Frankie's face grew pale with all the shouting and he went into the parlor to watch *Godzilla* on Million Dollar Movie.

"Look what you did now," Johnny said.

"No. Look what *you* did. I told you we were right last summer. I told you it had been enough. We let her stay and this is what happens. But don't worry. I'll clean it up. I always clean it up."

Having heard them, Lella wept in her room. When she felt herself running out of tears, she stared into the mirror and pretended she was Jennifer Jones just having been told of William Holden's death in *Love Is a Many Splendored Thing,* and wept some more. The salty drops finally ceased; she dabbed talcum powder under her puffy eyes and on the tip of her red nose in case anyone walked in on her.

Behind the frosted pane of the bathroom door, caked over with so many layers of white enamel paint that closing it completely was an impossibility, Dolores took a shower. She was a woman now. Baths were for kids.

From the parlor came Carla's whispers. She was talking on the phone to her sister-in-law Adrienne, Louie's wife:

"Adrienne, I just had to tell you. Dolores became a lady today."

☆

Johnny ate his two sunny side up eggs and slice of toast at breakfast the following morning while the children drank their eggnogs. Dolores did not go to school, however, nor did Carla go into work. Dressed in a black straight skirt and a white blouse, Carla put a kerchief over her hairdo so as not to have the wind disturb it. After eating a slice of buttered Italian toast which she dunked into a hot cup of coffee, she set out for Blessed Trinity.

At home, Carla told Dolores and Lella how she had presented herself to a confused Sister Aquinas who protested that she could not possibly be Dolores DiGiacomo's mother for she had spoken with her the day before.

"Apparently after eight years with this school, you cannot even remember who my children's mother is on account that your enrollment is filled way beyond its capacity," Carla had said coolly.

"Then who was here yesterday?"

"I have no idea. I've come to discuss my daughter as I was instructed."

"But the note said to come *yesterday*." Sister Aquinas pushed papers around on her desk. "I'll call for Sister Devine."

"There's no need for that, Sister. I want to pull my children out."

"But, Mrs. DiGiacomo, we have no quarrel with your other children."

"May I remind you, Mother Superior, I have one other child here. You really should keep better track of your sheep. I'll help you. As I said, I am withdrawing both of my children from Blessed Trinity. I've never been an advocate of parochial education. I only sent my children here because my husband desperately believed it would teach them respect."

Carla had leaned forward, torn off a blank piece of paper from a pad on Sister Aquinas's desk, and written with the nun's fountain pen:

February 4, 1962.
   I am hereby withdrawing my daughter Dolores and my son Frank from Blessed Trinity. Please forward their records to Shallow Junior High School and PS 48 respectively.
   Carla DiGiacomo.

"I'll wait for my son in the hall." Carla stood up.

"You're a foolish woman, Mrs. DiGiacomo. I'll pray that you realize your mistake."

"Don't waste your prayers on me, Sister. You made the mistake."

"Then me and Mom went to Roosevelt's and Mom got me a hot fudge sundae. She only had a cup of coffee and a danish," Frankie said.

"Now I can play stickball during recess. They never let us do anything in the schoolyard at Blessed Trinity."

Carla smiled at Frankie. Tears came to her eyes and she wiped them with her hand.

"What's wrong?" Frankie became alarmed.

"I'm just catching a cold."

"Do we have to enroll in PS 48 today?" Frankie asked.

"No. Lella can take you tomorrow morning." Carla fumbled in her purse for a tissue.

"Frankie, let's go to the movies." Carla suggested.

Lella felt slighted. Only she had ever taken Frankie to the movies.

Carla looked at Lella and Dolores. Lella waited for Carla to invite them too.

"Just you and me, Frankie," Carla added.

"Wow! Gettin' thrown out of school is great!" Frankie said.

In the middle of *The House of Usher*, Carla began to cry.

Frankie rested his hand on his mother's trembling arm.

"Are you frightened?" Carla asked.

"Are you?"

"She went to Lella instead of me," Carla mumbled.

Frankie stared at the screen while he patted his mother's sleeve to comfort her.

6

JOHNNY AND CARLA

On a warm Sunday afternoon in April, Lella carried a box of pastries from Alba's Pasticceria over to Regina and Aldo DiGiacomo's house for the christening. Johnny's sister Rose had given birth to a son. Lella walked in between Dolores and Carla, who held a plate of her famous rice balls. Johnny and Frankie led. Together, they all marched down Eighteenth Avenue.

While Rose helped Regina prepare for the christening celebration, her husband Junior attended the baptism. They had chosen Johnny's younger brother Tony and his Armenian wife Arpi (whom the DiGiacomos simply called *The Armenian*) as godparents.

"They won't wait for us to eat; they never do. Watch," Carla said.

"Don't start, okay?" Johnny pursed his lips; his voice went flat. It always went flat, expressionless, when he was uncomfortable or anxious.

"He's worried we'll be late and his mother will yell at him," Carla said to Lella.

"And you're miffed they didn't ask you to be the godmother," Johnny told Carla.

"Just once, once I'd like to see someone in your family make me the godmother," Carla said.

"I told you not to start," Johnny said.

"Didn't he start?" Carla turned to Lella.

"I'm not anyone's godmother," Lella said.

Carla gave Lella a look that said, why would she expect to be?

All of the homes on Regina and Aldo's block were private, some brick, most aluminum sided with postage-sized front yards bordered by hedges. With fewer people on the street than on Johnny and Carla's block, it was quiet. Away from the bustling commercial end of the avenue, it boasted of a park on its corner, albeit cement paved. The homes were attached by two's, each pair separated from others by driveways too narrow for modern day cars to fit into.

Johnny's family passed a crowd gathered in front of a house as they turned down the block. With a limousine parked out front and everyone smiling as they strained to see into the front door, Johnny's family knew a bride would soon be emerging.

"Let's wait for her," Dolores suggested.

"No. We're late," Johnny said.

"Dolores, just think. When you get married, the whole block will be standing outside to see you," Carla said.

"Were they there for you?"

"Of course."

"I don't see what's so great about seeing a bride." Frankie picked up a stone and aimed it at a car's tire, but Johnny grabbed his hand before it let go of the rock.

"Lella, if you got married, we wouldn't have to wait so long," Dolores teased.

"There are other ways to get a crowd to come to your door." Lella stared down at the sidewalk as she spoke. She had made her choice to live with Johnny's family. She would probably never get married.

"Yeah." Frankie jumped into the conversation. "Like the time that dog was chasing fat Joey Colavito and Joey was so scared he smashed right through the glass door of his apartment house. Boy, the whole block was there when they carried him out. You shoulda' seen the blood . . ."

"Basta!" Johnny stopped him from going on.

"I'm never getting married," Dolores said. Carla and Johnny exchanged glances of alarm.

"Why, Dolores?" Carla tried to be matter-of-fact.

"I just don't want to."

"How do you get married anyway?" Frankie asked.

"You meet someone — and you want to be with them all the time. It's fate. Your mother and I met in church. Sometimes it's somebody you've known all your life," Johnny said.

Lella blushed.

"That's not it, Johnny," Carla interrupted. "When you're ready, you make up your mind. You just decide to find someone, marry someone nice, start a life together."

"How do you know it's the right person?" Dolores asked.

"Run and kiss your grandfather," Johnny told Frankie.

Everyone knew that Johnny had first seen Carla at Mass one Sunday morning at Blessed Trinity. He had pushed the collection basket down her aisle and purposely hit her white-gloved hand as she deposited an offering. When she looked up, he smiled. At the close of the service, he waited for her in the vestibule and walked her home.

He absorbed her in conversation about literature and politics. He told her how, like herself, he had been a student in the Rapid Advance — done seventh and eighth grade in one year — and graduated ahead of time. After high school, he joined the construction company, where his father still worked as a carpenter, only to earn enough money for college. Then the war broke out. Now he was back at the company, waiting to enter school in the fall; he was going to be an engineer.

In the months that followed, he convinced Carla that he was her knight in shining armor. And although she said she married for love, all she could ever remember about her wedding day was the rain — it had been the wettest day of the year. Johnny's brother Louie had consoled her by telling her in Italian that the bride who got rained on was the lucky bride. He was a master at reinterpreting adversity with a simple proverb: if someone spilled wine on a white linen tablecloth, it was good luck; if they stepped in shit, it was really good luck.

The first vow Johnny broke with Carla was not keeping his promise to go back to school. She never forgave him, complaining she had been married under false pretenses. In front of Lella and the children, she accused him of settling too easily, requiring too little. When he became the owner of the construction company, Carla told Lella that if the business fell apart tomorrow, Johnny would be content to eat pasta and beans for the rest of his life, so long as he had his family.

Aldo sat in his lawn chair in front of the house. Johnny's older brother Louie sat beside him. Aldo held a pipe in his mouth with one hand; with the other, he used a match book cover to stir up the glowing shreds of tobacco as he took quick short puffs. He removed the pipe and exhaled a long cloud of fragrant smoke when he saw them. Lella knew that unlike Zi' Regina, Zi' Aldo liked Carla, the fact that she read, that she had opinions on things other than when the table should be set. His face was shaded by a large sign on a post firmly planted in the ground of his front yard: *Bill Ray Aluminum Siders*. It read in green and blue.

"Pa, you want me to take the sign down. You've been advertising for them for a year and a half," Johnny said, sitting down on the stoop.

"I tell Bill two years." Aldo held up his index and middle fingers. "Ven it's two years, I take it down."

Lella deposited the box of pastry on the kitchen table. Carla deposited her rice balls.

"Hot, always so damn hot and stuffy in this house," Carla whispered to Lella.

Lella looked around the familiar kitchen, immaculate, despite the huge meal that was being prepared. As usual, the heat was on, the oven going, and the windows closed, keeping the smells imbedded within the plaster walls, blending them into one ever present odor that vacillated between parmesan cheese and the new gray and white floral sanitase Johnny had just put up.

The checkered kentile floor was new too; Regina liked new. She threw out gilded mirrors and mahogany pieces for cheap blond finished plywood furniture that was in vogue. She relegated the oval portraits of her parents to the basement and hung a large amateur oil painting of George and Martha Washington at their inaugural ball over the couch.

Some things never changed, however, like the green and brown box from Ebinger's Bakery that sat perched on top of the refrigerator. Inside there was always a recently purchased yellow sponge cake with thin glossy chocolate icing that could be lifted off like a piece of plastic, leaving the dollop of whipped cream and the cherry perfectly intact at the center. In the dining room, a glass cabinet hosted a wide selection of colorful liqueur bottles. A bowl of realistically painted wax fruits sat on a lace doily in the middle of the kitchen table.

Regina removed a platter of vegetables from the refrigerator, and chose a seat nearest to the window to afford her the most light. She concentrated on a paring knife; her grip tightened around the handle, as she peeled celery strings from one end of the stalk to the other. Lella found a knife and dragged a chair over to Regina. She sat down next to her.

"I'll set the table." Carla said. She walked heavily on her high heels into the dining room, and the floorboards vibrated, causing the contents of the china cabinet to rattle.

"If the dishes come crashing down, I'll ban you from this house forever," Regina said in Italian to Carla.

"It's too early for the table anyway. They're not back from church yet," Rose told Carla.

Carla took her place at the table. She watched Adrienne and Rose stuff artichokes and grate cheese, and Regina and Lella clean celery. The women stayed away from the men; they always spoke about the business — Johnny filling Aldo and Louie in on the latest scandals and problems of the construction company. But, today, they were talking politics. Their voices carried through the screen door into the kitchen. "Und dis is how it begins," Aldo said about President Kennedy's having put ten thousand troops on alert in Okinawa.

"No, Pa. It's only an alert. It's just to scare the Communists in Vietnam. The U.S. won't make any moves," Johnny said.

"I tell you. Dis is just the beginning. By the time boys are big — "

"By the time the Frankie and Ralph are grown, this'll be long over. The world can't take another war," Louie said.

Talk of Frankie fighting made Lella nauseous. She was glad when Junior drove up with the new baby and godparents, and the conversation ended.

Carla got up to set the table.

"Now?" Rose looked at her surprised.

"Now," Carla confirmed.

Regina was about to summon the crowd outside when Joe Black, carrying a large fruit basket, burst through the screen door. Joe Black was short and fat with a bald head wider than it was long and an equally broad grin. Because of his bulging eyes and scratchy-sounding voice, the children called him *frog face*. Because he was extremely dark, the workers on the job had long ago name him Joe Black. Because his brother-in-law was the local mobster Jimmy Coconuts, he had gotten a job in Johnny's company. And because he was about to disrupt their meal, Regina cursed him under her breath, then smiled and said, *"Grazie,"* as she accepted the basket of fruit.

"Congratulazione, Signora," Joe Black said, complimenting her on the new grandchild named after Aldo. Then he proceeded to shake the men's hands and kiss all the women. When he approached Lella, he paused and grinned with such delight, Lella thought he would devour her right there in front of everyone. When he bent over Carla, she turned her face and lit a cigarette.

Joe Black appeared on every holiday and at every celebration to make *una buona figura*, to look good, to keep his job. Then, after a quick drink of Blackberry Brandy, he left, with his hand held high, foolishly blessing everyone as though he were the pope.

When he was gone, the procession began. Heaping platters of pickled peppers, artichokes, and eggplants; dishes of provolone, salami, prosciutto, hard sausage, baskets of crusty bread that cut the sharpness of the cheeses and vinegar were carried in by the women. Aldo brought up the wine that he had made from his own grapes, fermented in giant barrels, pressed, and stored in his cool cellar. He sat at the head of the table, the gallon of wine beside him on the floor, as though by controlling its distribution, he could control the entire scene.

Louie stood up and held a glass of the red wine high in the air.

"We welcome this new member of our family. We wish him health, happiness, and a strong pitching arm. I remind all of you children to always stay together like this long after Grandma and Grandpa, your parents, and even I am gone. *Salute! Cent'anni!*" They all raised their glasses. "A hundred more years," they echoed. "More days like these."

"Did you have to be so morbid?" Adrienne whispered to her husband.

"Oh, I forgot," he said, rising again. "If you know someone who needs a smile today, loan him one of yours. And . . ."

"Sit down!" Adrienne tugged at his starched white sleeve.

"You know you're just like your mother. The apples don't fall far from the tree." He held out his glass for Aldo to pour him another.

Adrienne covered the glass with her hand, fearing he would rise for yet another speech.

"Hey, Babe, a bird don' fly with one wing." He removed her hand.

Dolores and Louie's son Ralph sat in observance as the ravioli was brought out.

"This is just a rehearsal." Ralph leaned towards Dolores.

"For what?"

"Thanksgiving."

When Ralph and Dolores were little, Rose had stopped the cousins from going to the bathroom together one Christmas Eve. It had been their ritual. Lella defended them by saying that there was nothing offensive about this, no pulling down one another's underpants. While Ralph sat on the bowl, Dolores would entertain him with a puppet show from behind the clothes hamper, and while Dolores sat on the bowl, Ralph did the same. They had learned the routine from Lella who used it as a potty training technique for Dolores and Frankie.

"That's perverted," Rose told Lella.

"Wait a minute, you two. One at a time!" Rose had yelled when she saw them climbing the stairs together that Christmas Eve.

"It's time," Aldo announced, setting down his last leaf of artichoke. Johnny stopped peeling the orange he held; Louie bit down on the stalk of finocchio he had just dipped in seasoned olive oil; Rose put down the platter of veal birds she was about to bring back into the kitchen. They all knew what was to follow.

"It's time," he repeated. "Vee decide on the veek vee go to the farm next summer."

Carla feigned an urgent "call," and ran upstairs to the bathroom for what Lella knew was a smoke. When she took her place between Adrienne and Lella again, she was smirking.

"What happened to you?" Adrienne whispered.

"It's better than the fish story," Carla said, referring to one Christmas Eve when Regina was on her way home from the fish market and was seen running down the avenue after an eel that had escaped from her shopping bag.

"Tell me," Adrienne urged.

"Later." Carla put her hand over her mouth to contain her laughter.

"What are you talking about?" Lella begged to be included.

But Carla waved her off and shook her head.

At Adrienne's insistence, she told them how she had found Regina bent over the toilet, her fingers in her throat in an effort to purge herself. On the rim of the sink sat a smoldering cigarette. Carla had laughed at the sight of the revered woman stooped over a john, concealing not only the secret of what she considered to be a trim figure but the fact that she smoked to boot. *"Ma va fa Napoli!"* Regina had cursed her.

"How about a poker game," Louie suggested

They all dug into their purses and pockets for loose change, including Regina who had quietly returned to the table.

At home, Lella stayed up with Johnny and Carla, waiting to hear what Johnny's reaction to Carla's story would be. After the couple had retreated to their bedroom for the night, Lella stood by their closed door. Johnny dropped the loose change from his pockets onto the dresser and unzipped his pants; they got into bed. Then Lella heard it.

"Your mother smokes," Carla said to Johnny.

"I know."

"You knew?"

"Of course I knew. She thinks nobody knows."

"Then you know about the other thing."

"What other thing?"

"You don't know then!"

"What thing?"

"She makes herself throw up."

"Go on!"

"I swear. I saw her."

He shook his head in amazement: "Son of a bitch."

7

LELLA AND JOHNNY

Maybe it was in Dolores's reading *The Catcher in the Rye*, or in her listening to Bernadette Scoma's familiar refrain: "It's a man's obligation to perform an operation. He puts his bone-ation in a girl's separation to increase the population. Would you like a demonstration?"

But the summer Dolores bought boxes of Ritt dye and turned all her white undergarments into pink, yellow, blue, and Nile green, the summer Dolores turned fourteen, Lella knew that Dolores had learned what sex was.

From the window in Frankie's bedroom, Lella watched Dolores and her boyfriend Tommy B on the stoop every Saturday night as they listened to Murray the K's Swingin' Soirée on Tommy's transistor radio. They'd get a starry look in their eyes when Murray said that it was "submarine race boat watching time." Lella knew that meant make-out time, and she envied them.

Lella's eyes followed them down the block to the "secret stoop," the one covered over by a tunnel-like archway, the one from which they couldn't be seen. Lella wondered if all they were doing was kissing.

"They tongue kiss," Frankie told Lella. "I heard Dolores tell Bernadette. You know what that means."

"What?"

"A girl's willing to go all the way."

"Who told you that?" Lella demanded.

"Guys say it. They just know it."

Lella wasn't sure Frankie even knew what *all the way* was.

"Did you ever do it?" Frankie asked.

"Kiss?"

"Go all the way."

"What are you asking me that for?" she said, flustered.

But he looked at her hard with a smile on his face, as though he were trying to envision her in the act.

"Has the Good Humor man come yet?" she said.

When he laughed, she knew he understood what *all the way* meant, and she blushed.

On the evening of the fourth of July, the city became a combat zone with blasts of firecrackers, ash cans, and cherry bombs that would leave the neighborhood smoldering. Lella had been looking forward to going over to Johnny's brother Louie's because Louie had spent seventy-five dollars on Roman candles. But an argument ensued between Johnny and Dolores as to whether or not she should bring Tommy B along. When Carla began complaining about indigestion pains and said she would rather not go, Johnny got so aggravated, he decided the whole family would stay home. The day's heat of the past two weeks had been storing up in the flat tar roofs and turning the apartments into ovens at night. For days, out of open windows Lella heard the sighing, the tossing and turning of restless bodies. Some sought relief from fans placed in their bedroom windows, others, like old lady Yahtzbin next door (or the Retired Stripper, as the youngsters had named her) had taken to sleeping out on their front stoops.

On hot evenings Yahtzbin sprawled out across the steps. She wore nothing but an old pair of khaki shorts that resembled a giant diaper and held a rag to her flat chest in an effort to conceal two droopy breasts. During the day, she could be seen with her bare legs dangling out of her apartment window, clad only in the diaper and the rag. She did dress in winter, donning an old gray cardigan, a woolen skirt, a kerchief, a patch over her left eye, rags wrapped around her feet, and a pair of worn out canvas sandals. She carried a brown paper bag in her hand as she crept back from the avenue each afternoon. Frankie speculated that in the bag was a can of dog food, her meal for the day. When she reached her building, she would sit for awhile and, with the help of a large magnifying glass, read yesterday's newspaper that she had taken out of the corner litter basket, or smoke a cigarette, or just stare. She hauled enormous pails of coal into the alley to feed the furnace all by herself, unless Johnny was around.

"Let me carry those, young lady," he always offered, and took the pails from her.

Johnny was the only person who made her smile and caused her blotchy puckered skin to blush.

On that sweltering fourth of July evening, Lella watched from the second floor window as a pack of teenagers gathered on their bicycles in front of the retired stripper's house. It was attached to the DiGiacomos' building yet markedly separated from it by the pair of white stone lions on either side of the DiGiacomos' freshly painted red steps.

Joey Colavito from around the corner approached the group of kids. He was always so messy — overweight, sweaty, black T-shirt soaked with perspiration, half in, half out of his stained chinos.

"Sing for us, Joey," Frankie said.

Joey cast his blue eyes downward, and broke out into his rendition of the only song he ever sang.

"*Pretty little angel eyes, yeah. Pretty little angel eyes, yeah. Pretty little angel, pretty little angel, pretty little, pretty little, pretty little . . .* ," he began in his deep, off-key voice, one hand on his fat hip, the other snapping his fingers.

He was terrible. The rest of them burst into laughter. Lella laughed too.

"God damn, lousy kids," Yahtzbin cursed in a thick Russian accent.

"Hey, Yahtzbin, want a lick?"

Bernadette, who lived in Yahtzbin's apartment house with her mother, was straddling Nick's bike. She held out a popsicle.

"You know, Bungalow Bar tastes like tar, the more you eat it, the sicker you are!"

Bernadette's lips and nails were painted white, her hair teased up like spun cotton candy.

"Mind if we play stoop ball?" Nick aimed a new pink Spaulding at Yahtzbin. "One point for your head, two for your thighs, and bingo, three for your — "

With that, the old woman got up opened the door to her building some and slid her thin body through the opening. She lifted the sash of her apartment window and sent the pack scurrying as she emptied a pail of hot water onto the sidewalk, screaming, "God damn, lousy kids!" The gang tore down the street, colored plastic streamers flying wildly from the handlebars of their bikes, Bernadette's heavily lacquered hair unyielding to the wind. Empty Yoo Hoo bottles rolled for Yahtzbin to pick up.

As the group neared the secret stoop where Dolores and Tommy B were hiding, Johnny cried out for Lella. The ambulance he had called for was heading up the street. The teenagers turned around on their bikes and followed it.

Johnny got into the ambulance with Carla.

Lella and Frankie headed towards the secret stoop to find Dolores. Frankie told Dolores that Carla had been taken to the hospital; she was dying; Johnny was going to kill Dolores because he didn't know where she was. If Frankie and Lella had told Johnny she was making out with Tommy B, Johnny would have really killed her.

"Thank God!" Lella said, when Johnny phoned. "It wasn't a heart attack. Your mother's going to be all right."

"What was it?" Dolores asked, whimpering.

"Pleurisy. Probably from her smoking. All her coughing and this heat made her pass out. She was having these pains all evening — a sticking in her chest."

"Is she coming home?" Frankie asked.

"Not tonight. They want to keep her for tests."

"Can we go see her?" Dolores nervously curled a lock of hair around her index finger.

"We'll all go tomorrow. Tomorrow is another day." Lella was already reviewing her role as lady of the house, putting in order the tasks and responsibilities that lay before her.

When Johnny got home, he found Dolores lying on her bed on top of the covers.

"Where the hell were you? Your mother almost died!"

Lella winced at the degree of his anger.

Dolores sobbed into her pillow. Johnny grew calm and patted her head, and Lella understood that the seeds for Tommy B's demise had just been planted. Two days later, Dolores broke off with Tommy B.

Because Carla was running a low grade fever and complained about fatigue and joint pain, she was kept in the hospital and treated symptomatically. She attempted to leave on her own one morning but, when she stood, found herself too weak to move any further and slipped back into bed, resigning herself to an extended vacation in what Lella referred to as the germ motel.

Lella visited Carla every afternoon. When she returned home, she stripped off her clothes and showered for a long time. Johnny went to the hospital after dinner each evening and remained until visiting hours were over. Afterwards, he stopped at his brother Louie's for a cigarette and a cup for coffee. Home again, he collapsed in his favorite arm chair. With the television on, he read the *Journal American*, while Lella sat across from him and hemmed a skirt of Dolores's or sewed buttons onto Frankie's shirts. Though Lella tried to act normal, their conversations were anything but ordinary. As if prohibited to discuss matters of consequence in Carla's absence, they spoke of her condition and little else.

"Are you worried about Carla?" Lella asked one night, catching Johnny in deep preoccupation.

"No, no," he assured her. His eyes were on her hands, deftly working the needle.

Her white chenille robe opened slightly when she turned to pick up a new spool of thread. She ignored it at first, but then realized the open robe afforded him a partial view of her braless breast.

She sensed his discomfort.

He talked about work. She listened intently, wondering if she was displaying the helpless expression that Carla found utterly annoying, but that she knew Johnny responded to.

"I have to let twenty-five men go," Johnny said.

"Why?"

"Business is down. We didn't get the Hilton bid."

"How come?"

"Greco overbid. Now he says I've got to lay off twenty-five."

"Why doesn't he do it?"

"Because he owns more of the company than I do. Greco doesn't do dirty work."

"Do you know who's going?"

"I know who should go, but, hell, Sunshine's wife just had twins. It's the first steady job Lanese's had in almost a year. Stubby's got a bad back, but he's got a shitload of medical bills to go with it. He'll never get another job. Nino's my cousin. Then there's that lazy son of a bitch Joe Black. Eddie the Thief is Greco's cousin, and it goes on from there. I haven't said a word to Carla. I'm afraid she'll have another attack."

"Get some rest. You'll be able to think about it better in the morning." She noticed the robe open a little more as she shifted her position; she made no attempt to close it.

" 'Get some rest.' That's your answer to everything. I can't even close my eyes. God, I hate this crap. I should have become an engineer, like Carla wanted, or a teacher. She would like people to call *me* professor the way they do to that one downstairs. She would like to have been the *professore's* wife."

"You're good at what you do."

"You gotta be tough in this business, Lellie."

"You've done it before."

"I know. And it kills me every time."

"So what are you going to do?"

"Get some sleep," he said, smiling. "*Buona notte.*"

"Goodnight."

He left the parlor and went into the bathroom. Lella heard the toilet flush. When he passed through the parlor again, he did not look at her. He shut the door to his room. She wanted to go to him, say something that would make him feel better. Lella turned off the television and went to bed.

☆

Johnny did not go to Louie's house the following night. Instead he went straight home from the hospital and announced that Carla would be coming home the next day. Frankie took out the paints and a leftover roll of wallpaper. On the plain side he wrote: *Welcome Home, Mom!* and drew wildly colored flowers and hearts around it. Dolores baked a cake, then went next door to Bernadette's to spend the night. Just before he fell asleep, Frankie hid the sign under his bed so nothing would happen to it.

It was another hot and humid evening with no promise of relief. Johnny and Lella sat out on the front stoop with some neighbors. Across the street another group of people had gathered and were singing *Al di la*, while one of them strummed a guitar. Lella and the Professor's wife hummed along with them. The Professor went into his apartment and brought out bottle of *Chianti* along with some glasses to celebrate Carla's homecoming tomorrow.

"Will she be able to make the dance at the American Legion next Friday?" the Professor asked.

Johnny drank two glasses of wine, something he rarely did after dinner. His face was ruddy, his eyes twinkling the way Aldo's did when he drank too much. It was nearly eleven when he excused himself. He took one last drag of his cigarette, flicked the butt into the street, and headed upstairs. Lella followed.

"Did you figure out what you're going to do yet?" she timidly asked him.

"About what?"

"What you told me last night — laying off the men."

"Oh." He became despondent.

She had stupidly ruined his evening, she thought, in an effort to reach some point of intimacy with him. Now he probably wished Carla were there in her place.

He spoke softly to her.

"I haven't decided yet. What are my choices?"

He smiled, and she knew she had done the right thing.

"I guess I'll go to bed now. Tomorrow's a big day. I want the apartment to be clean for Carla," Lella said.

"The apartment is always clean."

"I mean really clean. I'm still finding firecrackers in Frankie's room, and I had only left the window open an inch!"

"*Buona notte*, Lellie."

She was disappointed. She thought he might ask her to sit up with him a little longer and talk the way they had the night before.

"*Buona notte*," she said.

Johnny watched the eleven o'clock news. Lella was already out of the shower and in her room when he turned off the TV. She could hear him completing his rituals in the bathroom — peeing, brushing his teeth, washing his hands. She remembered she had left her underwear, a pair of blue panties and a white bra, hanging on the towel rack. She never left anything out of place.

After the water stopped running, Johnny did not leave the bathroom. Lella imagined him picking up the cotton bra and cupping the empty molded piece of cloth in his hand, while his other hand fingered the thin lace border. She envisioned him bringing the bra up to his face and smelling, for the first time, Lella's smell — not her perfume, not her talcum powder, but her own scent — and becoming aroused.

Lella was lying down, staring at the street light outside of her window when Johnny, in nothing but his boxer shorts, appeared in her doorway.

"Johnny? Are you sick?"

"No."

"What is it?"

"I don't know. Too much wine. I couldn't sleep."

"Wine makes you sleep."

"Maybe it's everything else that's been going on."

"You want to talk?"

Her heart was pounding so she thought it might jump right out of her chest. Wearing only a thin nylon gown, she went to reach for her robe at the end of the bed. He stopped her as he sat down next to her on the edge of the mattress. He made no motion to leave; he just sat there, discreetly sniffing, searching for something.

"Johnny!"

He bent over her and took a deep breath. He remained over her, unable to distance himself. Lella lay frozen, frightened that he might be losing his mind, excited by his proximity. She reached up and touched his brow to test for some sign of fever. He was cool. She let her hand slide around his head down to the back of his neck where it rested. He kissed her forehead, then voraciously moved his lips down her face, sweeping over her lips and neck, down to the source of his attraction. There, he licked and sucked and smothered his face in the cushiony mounds.

"What are you doing?"

This was what she had always dreamed of, yet it must be wrong.

They were cousins. Still she did not attempt to push him away as she had Rosario.

Johnny was clearly on a roller coaster of excitement and she knew he could not stop, that he would say anything not to have to stop.

It's Johnny, she told herself. Not any man, but Johnny whom she had desired from childhood. She wrapped her arms around his head. Tonight was her last chance.

He pulled the sheet off of her then lifted the gown up over her arms and head with awkwardness that bothered neither of them. He kissed her torso and moved his mouth down between her legs where he licked, his arms extended above still grabbing those breasts. Before she had time to figure out what in the world he was doing, he lifted himself up and desperately tried to enter her. He eased himself in, pulling back each time she winced, until she could receive him completely. He pumped in and out of her with a frenzy. He cried out so loud, she became alarmed that he had hurt himself; surely Frankie had heard him all the way at the other end of the apartment. In a few moments, it was over. He slid out of her and, with his eyes closed and a half smile on his face, he rested his head next to hers. She waited for him to say something but he did not speak, did not open his eyes. He had fallen asleep. His weight rested so burdensomely upon her, she could barely breathe. She did not attempt to move him. She did not want to change the moment in any way.

It began to rain. She pushed him off of her, trying not to wake him for fear he would leave. She ran to close all the windows, and returned to bed. She watched him sleep until she herself succumbed to exhaustion.

The alarm woke her at six. Johnny was gone. She threw on her robe and ran to the kitchen to fix his breakfast. He was gone. She checked his room, then the bathroom.

"Damn him — " she cried. Why hadn't he given her the dignity of a short time alone before Carla came home? A time that would have assured her what she had done was okay.

Johnny picked Carla up on his lunch hour. Old lady Yahtzbin met them at the apartment house door and waved a yellowing pamphlet in Carla's face.

"It is your own fault you are sick, Mrs. Johnny. You eat that lousy Italian food. Pork. Ugh! You follow my diet here." She pointed to the printed information. "Skim milk. Goat cheese. Stewed prunes. You be healthy like me!"

"There's no need to talk to my wife like that just now, young lady," Johnny said softly taking the pamphlet from her. Yahtzbin lowered her eyes and pursed her lips. Frankie wanted to know if dog food was on the diet.

The Professor and his wife had been watching from their window. When Johnny and Carla passed by their apartment door, they came out into the hall and handed

Carla a giant bouquet of yellow gladioli that they said several of the neighbors had chipped in for.

Both Johnny and Lella tried to act normal, hiding any indication of the night before. Never looking one another in the eye, they were solicitous: he, compliment-ing her on the unexpected feast; she, jumping up and down to get more gravy, grate more cheese, clear away the macaroni dishes and put out flat ones for the roast. They weren't finished with their fruit and cake when Lella positioned herself at the sink and began washing dishes. Bernadette came to call for Dolores, Johnny re-turned to work, and Frankie, the only one who kissed Carla goodbye, went out to play ball, leaving the two women alone.

Anger and guilt had propelled Lella that morning into a whirlwind of nervous energy. She prepared the Sunday meal they had eaten even though it was only Friday, putting pig skin in the gravy the way Carla liked, and even making Regina's corn meal dish of *polenta* which Carla loved topped with gravy and sausage. Lella was sorry for what she had done behind her *comare*'s back: she would make Johnny pay for making love to her and then leaving her hanging like a used up mop. Lella would kill him by being kind towards Carla. And she would make him jealous.

Lella tried to decipher some sign from Carla as to whether or not she was aware of what had gone on the night before. Although Carla said nothing, Lella swore Carla did not look at her. Then, again, Lella could not look at Carla.

8

LELLA MAKES COFFEE

Rosario showed up at the farm early that summer, right after the last of the DiGiacomos arrived. When Ralph and Frankie sighted the trooper's car coming up the road, the unpacking came to a standstill. The bocce balls were set up; the chairs brought out from the shed.

Rosario was cordial to Lella who was not looking at him. His eyes followed her every move, taking in her thick auburn hair recently cut short and layered, like an artichoke, or her porcelain skin.

Observing that Johnny became aware of Rosario's gaze, Lella smiled and met Rosario's eyes head on with her hazel ones.

"What shall it be? Black or brown?" Lella asked, referring to the type of coffee the crowd demanded (brown meant American; black espresso).

"Black," they clamored.

Rosario followed her into the house.

Lella filled a pot with water and set it on the stove.

"I really did have a good time at the movies last year," Lella said.

"You don't have to be nice." Rosario took the can opener and began to cut the metal lid off the coffee can.

"I'm not. Really. It was sort of funny when you think about it."

Rosario stepped closer to her. As he turned the opener on the coffee can, the tendon in his arm became prominent. Lella remembered how it had felt being next to him, how hard and muscular his entire body was.

"Would you like to try again?" he asked, not looking at her.

She had never wanted to see him again, but the fact that he might make Johnny jealous made the offer appealing.

"How 'bout a pizza at Nino's tomorrow night? I'd suggest a movie, but I don't think I could take another broken window," Rosario said, and they laughed.

Lella spooned the coffee into the coffee pot. When the water on the stove began to boil, she poured it into the top of the espresso maker and the steam rose between them.

The following evening, Lella sat on a chaise lounge alongside of Carla and Johnny, and waited for Rosario.

"I don't understand why you're going out with him. You said yourself he was an idiot." Johnny held a pine cone in his hand.

"No, you did," Lella said.

"Leave her alone. She wants to go out with the guy," Carla said. "You don't like anyone she likes, not even Paul Newman."

"He makes me nauseous with those eyes of his glaring all over us," Johnny said.

"So take an Alka Seltzer," Carla told him.

Rosario was a perfect gentleman. When they crossed the road in town, he guided Lella ever so gently with his arm.

In the restaurant, a waitress with a bleached platinum bee hive and lots of makeup came up to the table and said hello to Rosario. When she spoke, her upper lip trembled.

"A friend," Rosario said.

Lella sensed they had been more than friends, for the woman uncomfortably stood in a corner at the bar, watching the couple's every move.

"Would you like to go to a movie tomorrow evening," Rosario asked.

Johnny pursed his lips and shuffled the deck of cards. Lella was waiting for Rosario. "Five card stud, one-eyed jacks are wild," he said to Carla, Louie and Adrienne.

"Looks like there might be confetti soon," Carla said.

"Somebody getting married?" Adrienne asked.

"It's only a date." Lella protested.

Carla pinched Lella's cheek. "We're just teasing." She threw down two cards and asked for another two in exchange.

The third night, Rosario took Lella to a state trooper's dance. Lella thought for sure that Rosario would show up in his uniform, but he was wearing a pair of white slacks with a black fitted dress shirt opened at the neck. Even Carla was taken with Rosario's appearance. Carla led Lella into her bedroom, and there, dabbed some perfume on Lella's neck. "Evening in Paris," she said. "Drove this sailor I once dated crazy."

On the fourth date, Rosario took Lella to a night club. He never took his eyes off of Lella in the black crepe sheathe with spaghetti straps that she had borrowed from Carla. Johnny had said it looked better on Lella, her breasts peaking out from the bodice, her sensuality nearly bursting the seams.

"You look fabulous," Rosario told Lella as the music act came on.

She liked Rosario's touch, the way he caressed her fingers throughout the performance. On the way home, he pulled over to the side of the dirt road. When he leaned over her, Lella did not resist him. She let him kiss her bare shoulders, and let his hands roam over her breasts.

☆

Lella couldn't wait to see Rosario again. They went to Nino's restaurant. The blond waitress was not there. Rosario told Lella he wanted to show her the fawn that he'd found on the highway earlier that morning. The mother had been hit by a car. Rosario decided to keep the animal in his barn. He let Lella feed it oatmeal out of a baby's bottle with a giant hole cut out of its nipple.

"What are you going to do with it?" Lella could feel the fawn sucking, drawing out the oatmeal.

"Keep her until she's strong enough to be on her own."

"Then what?"

"Turn her free. She'll never be happy here."

Rosario reached into his pants pocket and took out a small gift-wrapped box and handed it to Lella. She opened it and found a diamond ring.

"But I'd like *you* to stay, Lellie."

"Oh, Rosario. I can't."

"I don't understand. We may not know each other well, but we *have* known each other for a long time."

"About a day and a half in total."

"Look, we don't have to get married tomorrow. I thought you liked me."

"I do."

"Lellie, if you're afraid of something — you know, if you're ashamed of anything. I mean you're not a kid."

So he knew. Carla was right. A man can always tell, and he was willing to take damaged merchandise. In fact, he was being so understanding to her she wanted to cry.

How could she tell him she loved Johnny, that she had always loved Johnny, and that as long as he was alive, he would forever be in the way. Had she played with Rosario's heart worse than Johnny had played with hers? Had she led him on? Was she was a demon?

Rosario was talking, but she couldn't hear him. She wouldn't. She heard him say the word "go," and she nodded. She was destined to live in Carla and Johnny's shadow, and maybe that was her punishment. She would forget about revenge and be grateful for the life she had and for the DiGiacomos who had always helped her.

Rosario opened the car door for her. She silently vowed that if he wouldn't hate her, she would never go out with anyone else again.

Lella was standing at the stove in the kitchen, making a pot of coffee. Johnny sat at the table, picking at some cake. Carla took out a cigarette and a book of matches from her purse. She let out a loose cough as she tapped the filtered end of the cigarette on the table.

"Why don't you stop!" Johnny said.

"Why don't you?" Carla said.

He took out his pack of Camel's, walked over to the garbage pail, and threw the cigarettes into the can.

"I just did," he said, smacking his right fist into his left palm.

"Some of us aren't so well-disciplined," Carla said.

"You're always sick."

"You're exaggerating. It's fatigue."

"Quit your job."

"No."

"Get a checkup. I hear you at night; you have trouble breathing."

"I spent a week and a half in the hospital. There's nothing wrong with me. I'm tired, and I have a little arthritis. I'm not getting any younger and neither are you. We're married twenty years. You should be more tolerant of me by now."

"People don't become more tolerant of each other, Carla; they become indifferent. It's not tolerance you see around you. It's indifference."

Carla walked out, leaving the screen door to slam shut.

"Testa dura," Johnny mumbled.

"We're all a bunch of hard heads," Lella said.

Lella dipped the plastic measuring spoon into a can of coffee and filled the metal basket of the percolator. She wore a white linen sheathe that hugged her figure and revealed the even flow of her taut smooth skin from her face down to the plunging neckline.

Johnny stood close behind her. He was breathing so heavily her neck grew warm and moist from his exhalation.

"Smells so good," he said.

"Maxwell House."

"I mean you."

"I'm not wearing anything."

"I'm sorry, Lellie," he apologized for the first time.

She turned her head and looked up at him, as surprised as Johnny looked upon hearing his own words.

She said nothing. She replaced the lid on the coffee pot, went over to the refrigerator and put back the can of coffee.

"I've never forgotten what I did. God knows, I've tried." He followed her and placed his hand on her shoulder. Her groin began to ache.

She wanted to tell him that she had relived that night over and over again in her mind. She said instead: "I've been telling Carla that the smoking is going to kill her, but she doesn't listen to me."

Had he actually regretted being with her that night? Should she ask him? Lella wanted the warmth of his hand on her shoulder again; she wanted it all over her.

Johnny went out the door. The perking coffee grew darker each time it hit the glass bubble of the percolator.

9

EVERYONE HAS A SECRET

Johnny and Dolores climbed the hallway stairs. Johnny held the trunk of a seven-foot blue spruce vertically in hand. While they were gone, Lella had tacked a grouping of hanging silver bells on the apartment door. Johnny brought the tree into the parlor and placed it in the stand Lella had set up. Carla and Lella held the tree while Johnny lay on the floor and turned the giant screws that secured the trunk into the red and green metal stand.

"Your daughter wants to be a missionary!" Johnny said.

"She doesn't want to be a missionary. It's more like a crusader," Carla said.

"I don't want to be a crusader! I want to join Vista." Dolores grew impatient.

"Dolores, I didn't send you through four years of Barnard to go till fields like your great-grandparents did. What about art history?"

"It'll never be wasted, Dad. I'll always have it inside of me."

"Keeping it inside doesn't pay bills: it doesn't get you a clean job, Dolores."

"Dad, you can't always think about money. We have to give something back. We can't always be taking."

"I think you should go to graduate school. Get your Ph.D. Be a professor, marry a lawyer," Carla said.

"Sure. Be a perpetual scholar!" Johnny said.

"Be a nurse, marry a doctor," Lella said.

"Doesn't anybody think you should work?" Johnny groaned as he tightened the last screw into the trunk.

"I'm never getting married," Dolores stated.

"You know what the problem is? You kids have only known good times. I didn't pay sixteen thousand dollars to have you do in Apalachia what your ancestors did in Sicily," Johnny said.

Lella knelt next to Johnny and poured water from a tupperware juice pitcher into the stand's bowl.

"It's always Sicily he degrades," Carla said. "Your family didn't do so hot in Portaria either."

"The point is she wants Vista because she can't do anything with art history," Johnny said.

"You don't understand. The point is I have a right to make my own decisions and my own mistakes." Dolores went to her room and slammed the door.

"Now look what you've done and on Christmas Eve," Carla told Johnny.

"Better she cries now than *we* cry later." Johnny was crouched on two knees, sponging up the water that had overflowed from the tree stand with a towel Lella had handed him.

Lella returned to the kitchen and the *baccalà,* the cod fish she had soaked for days and was simmering in a red sauce with green olives as she did every year for the Christmas Eve fish feast at Regina and Aldo's.

It was Johnny's favorite. All week he would eat the leftovers for dinner, soaking up the sauce with a thick slice of crusty bread.

"What do you think about Dolores's idea?" Lella asked Frankie as he lifted the lid to the steaming pot and dipped a chunk of bread into the baccala's sauce.

"It's good," he said.

"You want her to go?"

"Sometimes people have to go. They have to get away, follow their dreams, or — "

"Or what?"

He didn't answer.

"Frankie, you're not thinking of leaving too, are you? People have to leave or what? What were you going to say?"

"Or nothing. Just nothing." He left the room, and she remembered the clippings, all the newspaper articles in his room about Alaska and the pipeline, and she said nothing.

Carla was running a mild fever on the day of Dolores's graduation. It was June, and Dolores had graduated Barnard *magna cum laude* in the class of 1970. When they got home, Carla put her achy body to bed, but not before she had made it a point to tell Lella that the younger woman had dressed inappropriately that afternoon and was too old to be wearing a mini skirt. The skirt was not as short as Dolores's skirt, nor was it knee length like Carla's. It was indecisively somewhere in between.

Johnny and Lella sat on the front stoop, sipping tall glasses of iced coffee. Frankie approached his father.

"I've been following a group of oil companies that are building a pipeline in Alaska. The job opportunities and the salaries are tremendous. Now that I got a high lottery number, I know the time is right. I'm gonna quit college," Frankie rambled on nonstop so that his father couldn't interrupt him.

"Forget it!" Johnny bellowed. "Forget it!"

Lella's stomach muscles tightened at the thought of Frankie leaving.

"Couldn't you finish school first?" she said.

"I can always go back to school. But I won't always be young enough to labor on a pipeline."

"Don't give me that crap. The men in your family are over twice your age and they're still hanging on girders!" Johnny said.

"But I'm free now. This is the time, Dad."

"Listen, Frankie, first you do what you *gotta* do, then you do what you *wanna* do, and right now you gotta finish school. You don't like engineering? Do something else. Be an accountant like my brother Tony."

"I can't wait, Dad."

"Frankie, don't do this to us." Johnny's voice was softer now as he stared into the dark brown eyes of his son.

"I'm tired of taking the damn train in and out of Brooklyn everyday like everyone else. The most exciting thing that will happen to me after school is I'll move to Manhattan," Frankie said.

"You understand, don't you?" Frankie turned to Lella.

No, she didn't understand why he would ever want to disrupt their lives together.

"Listen to your father, Frankie," Lella said.

Frankie shook his head in disappointment.

"No. He wants to go. Let him go. But *you* tell your mother, *tonight*," Johnny said.

The family gathered around Carla's bedside, like a scene out of a tragic opera, and Frankie revealed the plans of his new adventure.

"Of course it gets so cold and dark there all the time, people are depressed and alcoholics. But I think it's good that you're going. At least you're not paralyzed by your family the way your father is!" Carla sat upright supported by several pillows.

Lella rose to defend Johnny.

"You know sometimes, Carla, I don't even think you deserve Johnny!"

"And do you think *you* do?" Carla eyes turned red and bulging. Johnny grew pale.

"You! Who are you to talk to me about what I deserve?" Carla continued. "You, who would have been left in the gutter if it hadn't been for Papa!"

"What are you saying?" Lella said.

"I can't believe you're so naive you haven't figured it out by now. Don't you know you aren't related to the DiGiacomos."

"Don't, Carla!" Johnny said.

"Don't Carla me! She's not a child anymore. Your parents weren't Aldo's cousins; they were two dregs from his town who he didn't even know. And they didn't die either. They sold you. They would have sold you to anyone on the road if Aldo hadn't found out about it and bought you himself. That's how you got to Angelina and Gus. You were a present, but the DiGiacomos own you. They've always owned you."

Lella looked up at Johnny. Her eyes asked if it was true. His silence confirmed it.

"I'm saying you were sold and bought like a loaf of bread. I'm saying you have no right to talk to me about my husband. I gave you my home and my family. Now talk about deserving and tell me who deserves what!"

Lella's chest became heavy. Her lungs tightened, squeezing her heart until she thought it would stop beating and she couldn't take another breath. She needed air: she needed to be away from all of them. She ran out. Johnny went after her. When she reached the front hall, he stopped and let her make her way down the street. Dolores passed Johnny but he grabbed her arm and pulled her back.

"*Lasciala sta*'," he told his daughter to let Lella be, but she freed herself from his grip and went after Lella.

Johnny passed the slightly opened door of the professor's apartment.

"*Buona sera.*" Two meek voices came from behind the door.

Frankie sat dejected at the kitchen table; it had all been his fault. Left alone, Carla cried, though it was not clear for whom.

"Women!" Johnny poured a cup of cold coffee from the pot on the stove into a small saucepan and turned on the gas. "They get excited about everything. You notice how they always run out of a room. Where the hell do they go? They lock themselves in the bathroom. What do they do in the bathroom, I'd like to know."

"Lella's not in the bathroom, Dad," Frankie said.

"No. She's in Grandpa's bathroom."

"You think?"

"Of course. Where else would she go? She left her purse. Crazy women. The two of them. Your mother couldn't leave things alone." Johnny poured the scalding coffee into a cup and took it to the table where he sat next to his son. "You want a cup?"

Frankie shook his head. "She's right to be mad."

"You think she really never knew all these years?"

"Dolores and I never figured it out."

"Na, she knew."

"That's right. Stick your fucking head in the sand. Don't admit you could have been wrong."

"Don't you use that language in this house!"

"You all believe what you want to believe. You're out of touch with reality."

"Let me tell you something, young fella — something you don't know even with your 3.8 grade point average. Going off to Alaska to build some pipeline is reality? My foot! It's a pipedream! What do you kids want? Tell me. Never mind, I'll tell you. You don't know what you want because you've had everything. You've had it too damn easy. You can sit and mull over the world and analyze it with all your psychology courses as long as you want, but you won't change a thing. You know why? Because that's life. That's the way it is. It ain't easy."

"I'm not going because I'm ungrateful for what you've done for me. I just need to find myself."

Johnny dug his hand into his pants pocket and took out a dime. Then he slammed it down on the table in front of Frankie.

"Here," he said. "Anytime you have a doubt, call me. I'll tell you who you are!"

"You have to make a joke out of it."

"There are people who can always make something out of shit, and then there are others who, with all their money and education, all they do is talk and all they make is shit," Johnny said.

"Thanks, Dad." Frankie got up.

"And get a haircut!" Johnny shouted after his son whose hair brushed his shoulders. "They all walk out on me," he mumbled.

Johnny took a sip of his coffee; it was already too cold for his liking. He got up and dumped the rest into the sink. He went downstairs and sat on the stoop where he waited for Lella. It was dark when he finally saw her coming up the block.

"You look like one of them," she said, pointing to the two white stone lions on either side of Johnny. When she sat down next to him, her skirt rose and left much of her thighs exposed.

"Where's Dolores?" Johnny asked.

"She met one of her friends on the avenue. They went for ices. I should be angry with you."

"I just did what I thought was best — we all did. Although I hate to say it, maybe we were wrong."

"Zi — " she hesitated to call Aldo uncle, "Zi'Aldo explained it all to me. But you're right. I should have known. I felt so stupid when Carla said it. No matter how old I get, she makes me feel like a child."

"You're not a child, Lella. You're a lot wiser in ways than Carla. You're warm, and good, and — " he stopped. "Ah, Lellie. Sometimes it's confusing."

She wanted him to say it, to tell her that he would have liked her, not just for a lover, but for a wife. That his soul had been tortured thinking about her all these years. She only wanted him to say it, and she could wait an eternity until he did.

He followed so closely behind her into the hallway that she felt her A-line skirt brush his pants with every movement of her hips and buttocks. She could hear him taking those deep breaths, straining for something.

They found Carla out of bed in front of the television, sipping tea. *The New York Times Magazine* in her lap.

"How are you feeling?" Lella asked.

"Better. And you?"

"Better."

"So now you know," Carla told Lella.

"Now I know."

As Lella showered later, she heard sounds coming from Johnny and Carla's room — movement on the mattress, whispers. She put her head under the water to let the force of the shower beat down hard on the plastic cap and, like thunder, drown out the noise.

"Look at them," Frankie said to Dolores, as she stepped barefoot into the kitchen in the morning.

Frankie was watching his father from the kitchen window. Johnny, dressed in his painting pants and shoes, stood high on a ladder in the alley, touching up the green trim around the living room window about ten feet from his son. Frankie looked down at Lella who swept the alley. With sharp even strokes, never missing a twig, she made her way to the sidewalk. With brush and broom, they kept rhythm to the professor's wife's arias from *La Boheme* that came from the bathroom window below. They were smiling.

"I'm surprised she just doesn't get down on her hands and knees and scrub the damn sidewalk with a toothbrush. They're a trip." Frankie shook his head and laughed.

"I don't know why you think they're so funny." Dolores put a thick slice of Italian bread into the toaster. "They're out there as though nothing happened yesterday. Mom took a load of laundry down to the basement this morning. She was singing *Mamma,* that song about the dead mother, right in front of Lella. Can you believe it?"

"How'd Lella react?"

"She started singing with her!"

"Maybe we made too much about yesterday. Maybe it wasn't that important," Frankie said.

"They lie, conceal information, fuck around with somebody's life, then throw it up like a fit of indigestion after which they're completely calm and relieved, and we made too much of it?"

Johnny caught sight of his children at the window. He grinned and, raising his eyebrows in an exaggerated expression, held out his paint brush, offering it to Frankie and Dolores to help.

"Don't laugh at him, Frank. He's not funny."

"So what are you going to send me from New Mexico? That's where they're sending you, isn't it?" Frankie asked.

"A Mexican sweater when I get down to Juarez. Although you'll need more than a sweater where you're going."

"And what do *you* want?"

"A letter every other week."

Dolores and Johnny looked out again at Johnny and Lella.

Johnny dipped a paint brush into a gallon of enamel, then scraped it against the rim of the can, cleaning off just enough paint so the brush wouldn't drip. Both he and Lella did everything with effortless precision.

"When I'm finished painting, there's enamel all over the can and my hands are coated with the stuff. But Dad doesn't leave a trace — no turpentined rags lying around, no green spots on the concrete to give him away," Frankie marveled.

"They never wait until the paint peels, or the sidewalk gets dirty, or the gas tank of the car is near empty. They're always doing what they have to," Dolores said with disgust.

"What's burning?" Frankie turned away from the window.

"Shit! My toast! It's stuck in the toaster."

"How could you put this big piece in, Dolores? There's butter dripping all over." Frankie unplugged the hot toaster, flipped it upside down, and shook it over the sink.

"That's how Lella makes it."

"No she doesn't. She slices it thinner. She puts the butter on afterwards and melts it under the broiler."

Frankie stuck a knife in the toaster to dislodge the bread. Thick smoke rose up to the ceiling. Dolores went to open the window.

"Not the window! You want Mr. and Mrs. Clean to freak out? Open the door," Frankie said.

They stood with dishrags, fanning the smoke towards the foyer and out into the hallway like mechanics guiding a plane to its landing. Carla came running up the stairs with a basket of wet laundry ready for the clothesline.

"Something's burning!" she cried.

10

WEST OF BENSONHURST

Anchorage.
April 5, 1974
Dear Lella,

It's 2 p.m. on Sunday and still daylight! I like this part of the year here best because I know the darkness is almost over. I keep thinking about the beach. I could stand to stretch out naked on some hot sand.

We're almost finished with the first phase of the shopping mall. I've learned a hell of a lot about construction. Believe me, it's not only a matter of being in the blood!

Now I know why Dad wanted me to get a job inside of four walls. Sub-zero temperature is no fun. But I'm lucky I've had a job. The unemployment is growing here — everybody is coming looking for these $6,000 a month truck driving jobs. Still no pipeline. There's big controversy going on about using the land — a legal case headed for the Supreme Court this month. Keeping my fingers crossed.

How are Mom's aches and pains? Tell her I'd give anything for a bowl of her escarole and bean soup —

no fresh vegetables here. My relationship with Cynthia is over.

If the pipeline doesn't begin soon, I'll be out of a job —

Cynthia's father is my boss!

Sorry this letter is sketchy. I can't seem to con-concentrate lately. Give my love to everyone. Miss you all. (But don't tell Dad. Wouldn't want to give him the satisfaction.) Keep those care packages coming. The cookies were great. How about some pepperoni next time?

Love,
Frank.

Lella left the letter on the kitchen table for Johnny to read. Frankie addressed his letters home only to her. She had lured him into doing so by falsely telling him that, unlike Johnny and Carla, she finally understood his wanderer inclinations. He responded by saying that he wanted her, above all, to understand.

Johnny acted depressed that morning, but the letter seemed to raise his spirits. He was whistling, *I've Grown Accustomed to Her Face*, when he heard his brother Louie knock at the door.

"We're goin'!" Louie stood in the hallway. "Firenze, Isle of Capri, Amalfi Drive." He waved an envelope of airline tickets in the air. "August third. Four whole weeks. Not the best time, a little hot and humid, but it was the only month they'd give me off."

"Who's going where?" Lella came to the door.

"Italia, baby. How about some coffee?"

"Sure." Lella went into the kitchen.

"Got a letter from Ralph. Can you believe that son of mine signed up for another tour of duty? Getting drafted once wasn't enough. Vietnam almost killed his mother. At least he'll be stateside this time. Youth is wasted on the young!" Louie followed Johnny into the kitchen.

"Almost three years. Where'd the time go? Dolores called last night. Wants us to come out for Easter — meet this fella she's been seeing. He's a pilot."

Lella poured some coffee into two cups and set them on the kitchen table.

"Where's Carla?" Louie asked.

"Downtown. Big suit sale at Macy's," Lella said.

"Maybe we'll have some confetti soon." Louie put two spoonsful of sugar into his cup.

"Marriage? Dolores isn't even engaged," Johnny said.

"So this new *n'amorato* gonna pick you up in his jet?"

"He's Air Force. Besides, I wouldn't get on any plane."

"What? Drive all that way for a few days?"

"We just started that big hotel job. I can't go for any longer."

"You should fly. I can't wait for our trip."

"No way."

"What do you hear from Frankie?"

"He's building — for rich people. I didn't want him to do what I did. He should go back to college."

"Like *you* should'a. You were smarter than Tony, you know. But you were too eager to make a buck. The apples don't fall far from the tree."

"You got a saying for everything. Frankie don't write much, only to Lella. Calls occasionally. I don't know. We used to be so close."

"It's the times, Johnny. That's all."

They took the southern route. Carla sat in the front and navigated with her Triptik mapped out by Triple A.

"I don't understand why we couldn't have stayed in on of these cheap motels," Carla pointed at a billboard. "Only six dollars a night. After all, we have to get *two* rooms every night." Carla alluded to Lella as a burden, though no one had questioned whether or not Lella was coming; it had been assumed.

"I booked Holiday Inn all the way. My brother Tony says they're the best."

"*The best*. What does Tony know?"

"He drove to Florida. He knows."

Lella and Carla marvelled at the change in temperature and terrain and complained about the slow service once they got past New Jersey. They tried to imitate the different accents from state to state, and Lella refused to turn her watch back whenever they passed into a new time zone. She wanted to know what time it was in New York, that way she could figure out the time in Alaska.

Absorbed by the newness of it all, she never questioned whether or not they had locked the door or unplugged the appliances. She left her motel room early each morning, then sat in the motel's restaurant, sipping her coffee, giving others the impression she was traveling alone. Once they entered Oklahoma, the moaning began: long stretches of flat, dry uninhabited land; nothing in sight but the sky meeting the land wherever they looked.

"Doesn't anybody live here?" Lella asked as they entered New Mexico.

"There was a sign for a Boy Scout camp, but I don't see it," Carla said, unable to focus in on areas not delineated by concrete monoliths or square blocks. "There's no green. I like green."

"People must die a lot here being so far from hospitals," Lella said.

Johnny laughed.

"You could probably get to a hospital that was sixty miles away faster than going 'cross town in Manhattan during rush hour."

"I couldn't live here." Carla rolled down the window and lit a cigarette.

"Me neither," Lella agreed.

They turned off of the interstate and onto a small dirt road at the base of the Sandia Mountains. With the brown Sandias to their left, they climbed a different, green mountain range. Numerous clusters of small bushy pine trees made them feel less conspicuous, less vulnerable in the indefinite vastness. They glanced at one another warily as they passed through tiny villages: corrugated roofs on slanting porches, adobe houses with gaping holes in their sides, gray barns dried out like burnt logs, heaps of old farm machinery, skeletons of of old vehicles. Once in the town of Perano, they pulled up to the Gold Medal Bar as Dolores had instructed them. Johnny went in to phone Dolores; the women waited in the car.

"Should we roll up the window?" Lella asked Carla. Two cowboys in jeans with thick turquoise and silver belt buckles and string ties were strolling their way.

"Don't be ridiculous. Nothing happens here. It's too hot."

Dolores pulled up in her secondhand Datsun wagon, its orange finish faded from the sun.

"Oh my God," Carla said, when Dolores got out of the car.

"Don't say anything," Lella warned.

Dolores's face was fuller; she had gained a few pounds. Even her breasts seemed larger as, unrestrained by a bra, they bobbed up and down behind the thin covering of a yellow cotton tank top. She was obviously tanned, but no matter how her tank top slipped off her shoulder or her shorts rose, Lella couldn't percieve any tan lines.

Dolores kissed her mother, then Lella. Lella knew it was taking all the restraint in the world for Carla to refrain from telling her daughter that not only were her nipples apparent behind the flimsy fibers of her shirt, but the entire outline of her breasts. There were long threads hanging from her jean shorts that Lella herself had the urge to take scissors to. When Dolores hugged Johnny, he seemed oblivious to what made the other women so uncomfortable — the freedom with which Dolores moved about within her own body.

They followed Dolores in her car until they reached a cinder block structure she called home.

"I'll paint the place for you this week." Johnny was already calculating how many gallons of paint he would need.

"The owner wouldn't like that. Besides, it would just fade."

"But bare cinderblocks, Dolores?"

"I could have brought you curtains." Carla eyed the gold and brown printed fiberglass drapes that had clearly been cut in half to fit the length of the windows, and left unhemmed with threads hanging.

"I made these — well, I kind of recycled them myself!" Dolores said.

"Mom, you and Dad can have my room. Lella can take the couch and I'll sleep on the floor next to her."

"Maybe we should stay in a motel, Dolores," Carla said, noting that the bathroom had no door, and that the kitchen and living room were one big space.

"The closest one is fifty miles away. Besides, I want you to stay in my home."

"Whatever you say. After all, *you're* the lady of the house," Lella said.

"I can't wait for you to meet Scott," Dolores said.

"Is he Italian?" Lella asked.

"No. He's from Idaho." Dolores turned to Johnny.

"Dad, he did two tours in Vietnam."

"Where does he live?" Johnny looked around the small house as if expecting to find a naked Scott hiding under an ashtray.

"On the base! Kirtland. In Albuquerque."

Johnny nodded.

"His wife died of cancer last year. We're meeting at Garcia's Cafe at seven," Dolores said in one breath.

"He was married before?" Johnny cried.

Johnny nearly choked on his green chile enchilada at dinner when Dolores revealed her plans to get married on Easter Sunday, then move to Phoenix where Scott would do test piloting at Luke Air Force Base.

"Dolores, we don't even know his people!" Johnny exploded.

"I know *him*." Dolores lowered her volume, hoping her father would do likewise.

"*What* are you? What are your people?" Johnny asked Scott.

"A little English, a little Scotch, some French, a lot of Irish."

"Are you Catholic?"

"No, sir. Methodist."

"What the hell is that?"

"Dad!" Dolores scowled at her father.

"Who will marry you?" Carla asked.

"We've prepared our own vows," Dolores said.

"Just the two of you?"

"Father Jim at San Tomás will officiate."

"Father *Jim*?"

"Do you know the life expectancy of a test pilot?" Johnny asked Scott.

"I'm a good pilot, sir."

"Will your people be at the wedding?" Lella asked.

"My parents are dead. My sister can't make it."

"How can you live away from New York — the opera, the theater, the museums?" Johnny asked.

"*You* never go to any of them," Dolores said.

"But they're there, Dolores. They're *there*."

"To be honest, Dad, I don't think I could ever go back to New York. It's too congested, too dirty."

"Why can't you at least come back for the wedding?" Lella suggested.

Carla agreed. "Don't you want your grandparents, your aunts and uncles, your cousins at your wedding? Don't you want to give your father the honor of walking his only daughter down the aisle? Don't you want everyone standing outside of our house, waiting for you to come out? Dolores, are you pregnant?"

"No!"

"Someday, Dolores, God willing, you'll know what it is to be a parent. You think your grandparents will be around forever. You take away everyone's joy. You think only of yourselves. You hardly know one another. You want my advice? Don't get married," Johnny said.

"We're already married." Dolores lowered her eyes.

"You always drop bombs, Dolores, even on Good Friday!"

"Then why the talk of a wedding?" Lella asked.

"Because I *would* like my father to give me away in a church."

"You care so much, you couldn't wait," Johnny said. "You want my advice? Don't have children for a long while."

That's when they told him about Scott's three little girls who were spending the holidays in Idaho with his sister.

"I have grandchildren I've never met! You want my advice?" Johnny held up a shaking finger in one last frustrating attempt. "No pets!"

Carla leaned close to Dolores. "I always say, a woman should have something of her own to rely on — you never know if he'll leave you. I've always had my own bank account, put aside a little of my earnings each week. I have quite a bit for myself now. Are you surprised?"

Dolores shook her head. She was not surprised at all.

"One more thing," Dolores said to all of them. "Frankie's coming to the wedding."

While the little church of San Tomás lay quiet in observance of Christ's death — purple mourning cloths draped over its saintly figures — the DiGiacomo women labored, seldom getting in one another's way. Dolores sewed yellow gros grain bows onto her wedding gown, a white and yellow print peasant dress she had bought in a second hand shop in Albuquerque. Carla and Lella, in good humor and with expertise, opened package after package of necessities they had brought Dolores. They used up the entire supply to produce a meal for a hundred guests: the natives of Perano, Anglos and Hispanics who had been born there, who worked there, who would die there; the drifters — babyboomers who had come from east of the Rockies, seeking a less materialistic way of life, one that required little or no work.

Johnny agreed to see the small one engine wing plane that Scott kept at a private airport twenty miles away. Johnny consumed his usual breakfast of orange juice, two eggs over light, toast and bacon, and two cups of coffee. Scott waited at the door.

Johnny spent the rest of the day recovering. Lying on the couch with his eyes closed, he sipped ice water. Across from him, Carla sewed the traditional white money pouch into which the bride put all the cash gifts her guests lined up to give the couple. Carla had insisted on making it out of two of Johnny's handkerchiefs, even though Dolores warned her that nobody would give her any money.

"I don't understand why you went in the first place," Carla said.

"He talked me into it." Johnny pointed to Scott who was building a fire in the white kiva fireplace. "'How can something so small, toy-like, be threatening?' he tells me."

"In other words, he got to your male pride," Carla said.

"I figured hovering over the airport in that run-down contraption of his was a better way to experiment with flying than crossing the ocean in a jumbo jet like Louie's about to do."

"You mean you wanted to go back and tell Louie that you had ridden in a plane before him!" Lella said.

" 'Don't we have to tell somebody we're going?' I told him, and he slid this flimsy plastic window to one side and shouted to nobody, 'We're going,'" Johnny said.

Scott laughed.

"My stomach was going up and down like a roller-coaster so I tried concentrating on this one-inch cylindrical gadget on the hood of the plane, this piece of bent wire that looked like a straightened out paper clip coming in and out of a tiny hole in the cylinder. Every time the wire plunged, it went lower and lower."

"What was it?" Carla asked.

"Gas gauge. The lower it dipped, the less fuel in the tank," Scott said.

"And with that, he climbed higher!" Johnny took a sip of water.

"I figured since he was in construction — you know, skyscrapers — height wouldn't bother him."

"We do foundations," Johnny said.

"You did all right. You made it to the ground before—" Scott stopped.

"That's the first time I lost my breakfast since Quadalcanal," Johnny said.

The phone rang; it was Frankie. A storm was raging in Anchorage. All flights were cancelled; he would not be coming. Scott went back to the base; Dolores went for a walk. Lella washed the dishes. No one had seen Frankie in almost three years. He assured them he would be home for Christmas, but Christmas was eight months away.

"He told me he missed me. Can you imagine that?" Johnny told Carla.

"And what did you say?"

"Not much. I was so surprised."

"Well he didn't say he was moving back, so he doesn't miss you that much."

"So then they're both gone. Is that what you're saying? What happened? Both our kids ran away."

"It was probably your overbearing family."

"Maybe they left because they never had a mother to come home to."

"I never left my children alone!"

"They don't know who they are."

"Yes, they do!"

"Then who are they, Carla?"

"I don't know — but they know."

"We tried to understand them too much, relaxed the discipline, didn't teach them enough about respect. If anything happens to them — "

"What's going to happen?"

"So far away. Flying planes, working in the freezing cold, with strangers. Anything can happen."

"Nothing's going to happen. You're getting hysterical like your mother. I hate when you're like her."

"Scott's different. We don't speak the same language."

"Maybe you need to learn a new language."

"Admit he's different, Carla."

"He's different."

They took the northern route back: endless corn fields, familiar greenery, and mundane cities added to the numbness. They talked, trying to assimilate what had just happened. Dolores had been married off — twice — to a WASP about whom they knew nothing. She would be moving to yet another unknown place, and she, who had trouble sorting laundry, was now a mother of three.

Worst of all, she would live the nomadic life of a military wife — a few years here, a few there.

Scott had asked Johnny to take Frankie's place as best man. Since Lella stood up for Dolores, Carla was the only family member not to have a part in the ceremony.

"Only circumstance put Johnny at the altar with you," Carla reminded Lella.

Was Lella not entitled to a little pride? After all, she, too, had raised Dolores? Still, Lella guessed that seeing Johnny and her share a moment of intimacy with Carla's daughter must have made Carla think back on the day she and Johnny had tried to persuade Lella to leave, and must have made her wish they had been successful.

11

JOHNNY TAKES THE BELT PARKWAY

The week before Louie and his wife Adrienne were scheduled to return from Italy, Johnny took Carla to the hospital. She had been complaining of chest pains, a sticking in her heart, as she described it. Her bouts with bronchitis had become harsher and more frequent and her smoker's cough deep and hacking. Every morning, Lella heard her in the bathroom, the phlegm rumbling around in her chest with each effort to spit it out. She wanted to turn her upside down and shake the invasive mucus from her. After four days in the *germ motel* she was diagnosed as having pleurisy with early signs of emphysema, and was ordered to quit smoking. The pain in her joints and the fatigue she battled was not out of order, she was told, for a hard-working forty-seven-year-old.

Dissatisfied with methods of modern medicine, and cross about having to give up nicotine, Carla was anxious to go home. She felt uncomfortable leaving Johnny and Lella alone this time.

In one of her nightmares, Lella sprinkled cyanide in the Parmesan cheese. After one bite of *penne*, Carla suffered a horrible squeezing in her chest until she could no longer breathe. Suddenly, Johnny and Lella were engaging in torrid lovemaking which Carla watched from her casket placed (out of respect) at the foot of their bed.

A blue Camaro was tailgating Johnny's new Chevrolet on the Belt Parkway. The Camaro finally passed Johnny, nearly hitting a Volkswagon Bug as it slid into the fast lane. It pulled out in the stretch like a racehorse and ended up back in Johnny's lane, several car lengths ahead. Then it swerved into the right-hand lane and exited around Cross Bay Boulevard.

"God damn weaver!" Louie, who sat in the passenger seat, had said. "Guys like that think if they're not passin' everyone, they're not movin'."

But, as Johnny approached Flatbush Avenue, he saw the Camaro coming back onto the parkway. It did not stop and wait for a lapse in traffic to enter; rather it sailed non-stop, taking its chances as though playing some sort of Russian roulette.

"Watch it, Johnny!" Louie yelled.

Before Johnny could even turn the wheel, the Camaro's nose dove right into the front passenger seat, causing the Impala to head left in the middle lane of on-coming traffic. There it was hit by a second car.

Louie was killed instantly. Johnny's head went through the windshield. He could not stay conscious long enough to know that Carla had squeezed his hand in the emergency room and Lella thrown her arms around him.

Both caskets were closed out of respect to Johnny's disfigurement. The room at the funeral parlor was lined with enormous floral arrangements on stands, with cards that read like advertisements: St. Bartholomew's High School, or The Chase Manhattan Bank. They came from the men working on various jobs in the construction company.

For three days Aldo DiGiacomo sat facing his sons who lay side by side. Sometimes he wept uncontrollably, other times, silently, tears streaming down his face. When a new mourner knelt in front of the bier, Aldo's facial muscles constricted in an apparent effort to brace himself for their impending offer of condolence that would be given first to him, then to Regina, and lastly to Carla and Adrienne, all seated in a row to his right. Lella, Frankie, and Dolores, who had come to New York alone, sat directly behind them along with Louie's son Ralph.

With each murmur of regret, with each utterance of the word *coraggio*, Aldo said that courage was the most useless attribute now, and that he could not accept that his boys had returned unscathed from two fronts of a world war only to be massacred by a stupid nineteen-year-old who chose to play God with the lives of Aldo's sons. "Mamma," the old man called to his deceased mother. "Mamma."

Lella got up and knelt beside the old man, and held his hand.

Joe Black and his brother-in-law Jimmy Coconuts, wearing dark glasses indoors so as to appear inconspicuous, also came to pay their respects. Solemnly seated in the last row for two hours, they didn't utter a word.

When the family returned to the house each afternoon during the wake, hungry for the meals brought in by neighbors and relatives, Aldo took his designated seat at the head of the table. A bearded twenty-four-year-old Frankie sat to Aldo's left, a uniformed Ralph to his right, each taking their fathers' places. Although he normally picked a fight with Regina over nothing more than an extra piece of chicken put in his plate, the thunderous shouting was gone. He finished eating and cast up his tensed hands in despair, fingers spread apart like twigs on the branch of a barren tree, and retired to the porch where he remained until it was time to return to the funeral parlor for evening calling hours.

Lella warned Carla that it was too soon, that she should not be disposing of Johnny's possessions so quickly, but the day after the burial, she went through the apartment in a frenzy, throwing into boxes anything of Johnny's she found. Lella wailed and cursed God while she followed Carla around salvaging an article of clothing here, a tool there. In two days, it was all done, picked up by the Salvation Army. Carla sat down in the parlor and picked up the *New York Times* crossword puzzle.

Dolores had tried to dissuade her mother but Carla would not hear it. All Carla's previous compulsiveness was nothing compared to this. It was as though she were unleashing energy stored up inside of her for a lifetime.

Dolores then attempted to work with her mother, but Carla complained: she was either in the wrong drawer at the wrong time, moving too swiftly or too slowly, not folding garments properly, talking too much, or not talking at all. When Dolores questioned her mother's physical safety now that Johnny was gone, all hell broke loose.

"You think I can't take care of myself?" Carla snapped.

"It's just that burglars are more wary when there's a man in the house. And there are the tenants to deal with, the building to maintain. Daddy did all that."

"You think this family can't exist without your father? He's all you've ever cared about. Him and Lella."

"Because they let me. I can't get near you. I can't do anything right."

Dolores walked out of the room; Carla stood unmoved, as though her soul had shut down.

The following morning Dolores hugged Lella goodbye; she kissed her mother on the cheek. Frankie drove Dolores to the airport in a car his Uncle Tony had loaned him.

For awhile Carla's home was in a constant state of entertaining with friends and relations visiting every evening and all day Saturday and Sunday. Frankie met second and third cousins he had not seen since childhood, and there were always neighbors and men from the construction company.

Lella kept the apartment stocked with coffee and cake. After dinner she quickly cleared the dishes and put the coffeepot on in anticipation of the company which would start to arrive around seven. They would sit in the parlor and offer their regrets, talking about how much they had loved Johnny, reminiscing about the good deeds he had done for them when they were children or the jobs he had given them when they were out of work. He was a fine neighbor, kept his property neat as a pin. Then they would go into the kitchen for the cake and coffee. There, somber tones could not help but evolve into laughter and anecdotes about the living. Lapses in conversation brought Johnny to mind and heads bowed not out of reverence but discomfort.

In two or three weeks it was all over except for Johnny's brother Tony who made it his business to visit Carla and Adrienne once a week. Carla refused to step into Aldo and Regina's home after the funeral. She offered no excuses, except that she had dutifully visited them every Sunday for twenty-six years, and she was now going to do what she pleased.

Carla went back to work five days after Johnny's death. Frankie went through his father's files which amounted to a mass of papers in a brown manila envelope tied up with green string. He paid visits to banks, insurance companies, brokerage firms, the social security office. In the evenings Frankie recounted the events to Carla who relied on her son's judgement. Carla remained a paradox to Lella: she had always been so concerned with financial security and earning her own living, and even taken an interest in women's liberation. But she wanted no part of settling Johnny's estate. She only wanted it settled.

Lella poured her energies into Frankie, nurturing the man whose appetite had grown along with his muscles from physically laboring and lifting weights in his spare time. The evenings, however, were most difficult for her. She awoke at night and got out of bed. She crept into Frankie's room, picked up from the floor or a chair any clothing that he had worn that day, and went into the basement to run a wash. From the kitchen window out into the dark she hung the clothing on the line. She returned to bed for awhile, then rose at dawn to press, fold, and return Frankie's clothing to his room before he awoke.

Frankie bought a yellow Mustang and offered to teach Carla how to drive. She declined. Lella, however, wanted to learn.

Each morning Frankie and Lella set out for Blessed Trinity parking lot. Lella almost never went from first gear to second without stalling the car, and when she did manage to shift, the car jerked back and forth violently. He finally took her out onto the street and told her to do the best she could. The pressure of driving with other traffic kept Lella's jerking to a minimum. She had just made a smooth downshift and was shrieking with delight when they came to a red light at the top of a hill. The cars packed up behind her, but when the light turned green, Lella could not go from first gear to second without letting the car slide backward. The driver of the vehicle behind leaned on his horn and shifted into reverse, causing a series of horn blowing and downhill gliding. Frankie jumped out of the passenger seat and ran around to the driver's side. He opened the door, shoved Lella over to one side, and took the car to level ground. When he pulled over to the curb, they broke into laughter. A month later she took her road test.

"He didn't like me," she said of the inspector.

"You passed a blinking red light."

"I slowed down and proceeded with caution."

"You're supposed to stop."

"He didn't like me."

On her second try she received an automatic failure for having forgotten to bring her permit along. The third time she passed.

Frankie and Lella drove over to the ice cream parlor and shared between them a Mount Vesuvius — five scoops and toppings in one dish in the middle of the table. Frankie ate most of it.

"I can't understand you," Lella said, as Frankie tried to talk with his mouthful of pistachio ice cream and marshmallow sauce. He swallowed the entire lump and a sharp pain shot up to his temples. He winced.

"I said I'm moving out."

Her spirits plummeted.

"You're going back," she said.

"To Alaska? No. I got a one-bedroom in the Village. I'm going to work for Uncle Tony. If I like it, I'll get an accounting degree."

"What does your mother say?"

"It won't be fun being side by side with my uncle all day; he's not as easy going as everyone thinks."

"I thought you were studying psychology."

"I was. But my father would have liked me to work with Uncle Tony — he respected Uncle Tony."

"I was getting used to having you home again."

"Well, you don't want me to end up like that Rosario guy, do you? A grown man living with his mother."

"He married a waitress from Nino's."

"No kidding! You're not upset about that?"

"Sometimes I ask myself, what if?"

"Don't. He was an asshole."

"Maybe he was my only chance."

"Jesus Christ, Lella!" She grew uncomfortable as his eyes fixed themselves on the two mounds that molded her white mohair sweater.

"Have you ever seen a picture of the Grand Tetons?" he asked.

"Who are they?"

"Enormous snow-covered mountains in Wyoming."

She felt a rush of heat pass through her. She looked away from his familiar dark eyes and changed the subject."You know I'm thirty-seven. I can't believe it. I feel as though I just came to live with you, like I'm still a teenager." She watched a young couple sit down in the booth across from them.

"You look like a teenager."

"Your mother says Italians stay young longer because of our skin; we don't whither away like English and Irish women."

"Now that's probably true. You should have seen Cynthia's mother. Cynthia was the woman I was seeing in Alaska."

"I know."

"Her mother looked like she was eighty!"

"And Cynthia?"

"She was pretty, but whenever I think about her, I convince myself that in twenty years she would have wound up shriveled just like her mother."

Lella had stopped listening to Frankie. What was she going to do when he left? Carla didn't need her; she never had. It was Johnny and the kids she really kept things nice for. Soon they would all be gone and she would remain like a child in a deserted doll house with nobody left to play with.

12

FRANKIE MAKES DINNER

Carla and Lella stepped out of the elevator and marched down the narrow corridor of Frankie's new apartment house. Like the Magi, laden with shopping bags and stacks of pastry boxes tied up in string, they came bearing gifts for their beloved male child.

"Which way is the kitchen, Frankie? We brought dinner." Carla looked around.

There was a foreign smell coming from the archway that led to the galley kitchen.

"Smells good." Lella followed Carla into the kitchen where they deposited their packages.

Carla lit a cigarette.

"Do you have to here?" Lella knew Frankie hated to see his mother smoke.

"So what's cookin'?" Carla ignored her.

"Curried vegetables. It's Eastern," Frankie said, casting a disapproving eye at his mother's cigarette.

"We know." Carla flicked her ashes into a jar lid lying on the counter.

"Frankie, how long has this been simmering?" Lella removed the lid from a large aluminum pot.

"A few hours."

"Put the dishes away. We can drink it."

"Overdone?"

"Not if you wanted V-8 juice." Lella said.

"And I was afraid the rice might be gummy."

"It is," Lella admitted.

"Don't worry," Carla took a long draw on her cigarette and put it out. "We brought some eggplant parmigiana and veal cutlets. Take out the lettuce; we'll make a salad."

"I wasn't planning on salad."

"No salad?" the women said.

"There's a vegetable stand on the corner; I'll run down and get some."

"Don't bother, Frank. This is fine," Lella said.

"I have to move the car anyway. I'm parked in a tow zone."

"Pick up a nice red pepper too and a loaf of Italian bread. I saw a cute bakery around the block," Carla shouted after him.

When he returned, a familiar smell had overtaken that of the curry. Lella was holding a brass-framed snapshot of Dolores's family.

"Have you heard from Dolores?" Lella asked Frankie.

"She sent me that picture for my birthday."

"They look so happy," Lella said.

"Did you have to buy the frame?" Carla asked.

"No, *Mother*. It was part of the gift."

"Well, I'm glad you trimmed that beard you came home with. You ought to shave the whole damn thing off," Carla said as they ate.

"I think he looks handsome — mature." Lella gave a tug to the whiskered chin.

"Of course he looks handsome," Carla said. "He's a handsome boy. But that beard just hides his face. He'd be even more handsome without it." Carla blotted her lips with her napkin and placed it back on her lap, satisfied with the meal she had just eaten as well as the statement she had made.

"Ladies, could we not talk about me as though I weren't here?"

"If we're insulting you, maybe it's time to leave." Carla stood up.

"Come on, Ma."

"We haven't had dessert yet," Lella said. Why did Carla have to ruin everything?

"I don't want to say anything else wrong," Carla said.

Frankie looked to Lella who shrugged her shoulders indicating that's how Carla was nowadays. Then she also got up.

"I'll phone you, Ma," Frankie called as the two women made their way back down the long hall.

Carla never apologized for her swift exit. But then again, they were not an apologetic people. The following Sunday Frankie dropped in on his mother in time for the large afternoon meal. Carla was pleasant. After dinner Lella cleared the table, but when Frankie swept under the table the way Johnny used to, Carla got angry.

"Leave it!"

"Why?"

"Just leave it, Frank!"

"Hey, let me take you ladies to the movies," Frankie said

"*The Exorcist* is playing at the Walker!" Lella said as she filled the sink with soapy water.

"I don't feel like a movie. You two go." Carla put her feet up on another kitchen chair.

"Come on, Ma. Two hours. You love Lee J. Cobb."

"I'm tired, Frankie, and I don't feel like crowds."

"You don't mind if we go, do you?" Lella said. She was glad to have the time away from Carla — and alone with Frankie.

"Have fun." She waved her hand, urging them to leave her.

They shared a giant buttered popcorn, as had been their custom. Lella cut the last piece in half with her nail, remembering how Frankie would cry if she ate the whole thing. This time he offered to buy her another bag. She asked for a Coke instead. Frankie returned to his seat just as Jason Miller fell out of the window and down a long flight of stone steps to his death. Lella turned her face into Frankie's shoulder and squeezed his arm. It was like a rock, and she sensed he was purposely flexing his muscle. None of the hours he had worked out with weights in the basement as a teenager had produced the body that laboring in heavy construction had. When Frankie worked summers with Johnny, he had been given such menial tasks there was no effect on his physique. She wanted to poke at him all over, to test the extent of this makeover. She lifted her head up and settled back into her seat. After the movie, they stopped for coffee at the ice cream shop.

"How do you think they made her head spin around?" Lella took a sip of coffee.

"Trick photography."

"I used to love horror shows. They never frightened me at all. Now I can't stand to see a really scary thing."

"I noticed."

"Why do you think that's so?"

"Probably because you know how threatening real life can be. You don't want any surprises. Who wants a bad thing to happen?"

"Did you learn that in psychology?"

"It's common sense."

"Oh." She looked down.

"I didn't mean it to sound like that, Lellie."

"You should go back to school."

"Education isn't everything, Lellie. Dad knew that."

"It's a sin to waste a good mind. Look at your mother. Why do you think she's so frustrated? She's always resented the fact that she couldn't go to college."

"If she had really wanted to, she could have gone. She didn't need to work; you were home with us which is another thing that pisses me off. They should have sent you to school instead of wasting your time."

"It was what I wanted to do."

"Why don't you go now, Lellie?"

She laughed.

"I'm too old! Although I don't feel old. But I've always thought I was supposed to be."

"I dated a lot of women in their thirties — well, a few."

"Why?" Didn't men want those adolescent waif-like creatures she saw in fashion magazines?

"I like older women. They know what they want."

Lella felt the heat rising again.

"I've missed going to the movies with you," Frankie said.

"Was Cynthia my age, I mean old?"

"Younger than me."

"So what happened?"

"I was so nuts about her. She was different than any girl I had ever met in Bensonhurst — and that was the problem. That's why she broke it off."

"I'm sorry."

"Don't be. I was trying to fit in where I didn't belong. It's hard to figure out when you should compromise and when you should hang it up. Her family was weird, like they had some gaping hole inside of them they were trying to ignore. I wasn't comfortable with them. Ice people."

He shuddered.

"Because of the weather?"

"Maybe." He laughed.

"She wasn't Italian?"

"Shit, no. English and Danish. Her father had actually been born in Alaska. Her grandfather had been some big time lawyer. Made big bucks. She used to ask me what Italians ate, did for amusement. At first I thought it was a kick."

"You miss her."

"My ego does."

"I don't like to think about you unhappy with people like that."

"That's why I'm home. But I still want to build the pipeline. If they ever pass that federal right of way permit, I'm going back. You want to come with me?"

"Oh sure. I already wear two pairs of socks to bed in the winter!" She slapped her hand down over his and kept it there. "You know Sid Hyman?" she said, consciously removing her hand.

"The one who owns Toyland?"

"Yeah. He asked me if I wanted a job."

"Great! You're going to take it, I hope."

"I think so."

"Let's celebrate!" He called over the waitress and ordered a Mt. Vesuvius.

"Frankie, it's only a job in a toy store."

"I don't care what it is. You're getting out of the house."

As they walked home, her arm firmly hooked around his, they passed a man about Frankie's age, thin, with a long nose and a space between his two front teeth.

"Hey, wasn't that Tommy B?" Frankie turned around to get a second look.

"Couldn't be. Tommy B was killed in Vietnam."

13

LELLA VISITS ALONE

Lella cleaned the apartment, picked up groceries on her way home from work, helped with the laundry and cooked. On Saturday afternoons she visited Frank. Carla's mood swings were becoming insufferable and Lella, as well as Frank, enjoyed their time without her.

Carla invested in a secondhand car for Lella. She had grown accustomed to being driven most places by Johnny. The phone had begun to ring regularly at eight-thirty a.m., after Carla left for work but before Lella did. It was Frankie, settling into his desk at his Uncle Tony's accounting firm on Madison Avenue.

When Lella drove the car into Manhattan to see Frank, she told Carla she was going out with one of the salesmen from Toyland. If Frankie had no evening plans, Lella would invite him to an early movie so that she could find her way back to Bensonhurst before it got dark.

"Just checking in," he would say.

Each with a cup of coffee in hand, they chatted. The calls became part of the morning routine to Lella, like fastening her bra, like blotting her lipstick.

Lella took books out of the library — *The New States: Alaska and Hawaii* and *Blazing Alaska's Trails* — so that she could talk to Frankie about his dreams.

"Am I taking up too much of your time?" she asked him one Saturday.

"I hate when you say stuff like that," he answered.

☆

Thanksgiving found Carla in bed. Lella and Frankie were sure she had feigned that days' aches and pains so they would not even try to talk her into going to Regina and Aldo's.

The coffee and pastries were taken out, then put away at the DiGiacomos. Tony took out the deck of playing cards. Rose washed the demitasse. Frankie went over to Lella, who was sweeping off crumbs from the white tablecloth, and whispered that *Murder on the Orient Express* was playing in the city. If they hurried, they could catch the nine-fifteen show. A hesitant Lella narrowed her wide eyes.

"How can we leave? We haven't had snack yet?"

"That's not until after the poker game."

Frankie turned to Regina who was cleaning out her large black pocketbook for spare change.

"We have to go now, Nonna."

"*Ma* so soon?" Regina snapped the gold clasp of her change purse shut.

"I have tickets to a show."

"A show? On Tanks-a-giving?"

"Thanks for everything, Nonna." He kissed her cheek.

"You leave for a show?" The old woman was baffled.

Lella kissed Regina and Aldo. Frankie handed her her coat. Taking her arm, he pulled her out the door.

After the movie, they went up to Frankie's apartment for tea.

"Frankie, this was a crazy idea! How am I going to get home? I can't take the subway at this hour?"

"I'll drive you."

"You won't get back until two in the morning."

"So?"

"Why don't you stay over at the house and leave early in the morning?"

"I'd rather come home late than face all that traffic tomorrow."

She sat on the couch, her stockinged feet to one side of her. The lamp which had a red handkerchief draped over the shade cast a rosy tone over everything.

"You always had the most beautiful skin," Frankie said. "Must be those Mediterranean genes we talked about."

"Or that rag you have covering the light with."

They laughed.

He reached over and touched her cheek. She was grateful for the gesture and aware of the tiny lines that formed at the corners of her eyes when she smiled. She brushed the hair off his forehead the way she used to when he was a child and she'd put him to bed. Her hand slid down to his neck; she moved closer to him. Then she kissed him, but not the way she used to.

He gently pushed her away and sat with his hands folded between his knees. He dropped his chin to his chest and took a deep breath. Then he looked at her. "What are you doing?" he whispered.

"I don't know." The feeling was back, the one she had felt with Johnny and Rosario — the gnawing in her groin, the racing heart. "I have to go home now."

He got up and took her back to Bensonhurst.

When she came home from work the next evening, she found Frankie sitting at the kitchen table reading the newspaper.

"For God's sake, Frank! You scared the hell out of me!'

"Sorry."

"How did you get here so early?" she asked.

"I took the day off. I got home so late last night, I couldn't wake up this morning."

"It wasn't that late for you."

"I didn't sleep all night. We need to talk."

She took off her coat and hung it up in the hall closet, then went into the parlor and raised the temperature on the thermostat. She began to pull down the shades.

"I said I have to talk to you. Will you please sit down."

"You want some coffee?" She stayed by the stove.

He shook his head.

"Lellie, I've been thinking. I was wrong last night. Confused."

"Me too."

"Well, I'm not confused anymore."

He went over to her and put both hands around her face. He was so close he could hear her heartbeat, but she quickly disengaged herself.

"I don't understand," he said.

"Last night I made a mistake."

She hadn't slept the night either, trying to rid her body and spirit of the evil side again — the side that made her want what she couldn't have. Was she being humiliated by a DiGiacomo man, once again?

"Come on, Lellie. I'm not a child anymore."

"No, you're not. All day I felt guilty. Then it dawned on me — what was really going on. You, acting so innocent. As though what I did was so out of the blue, so unexpected. I know about signals — *vibes*. And I know what I've been getting from you."

"You're right, Lellie. That's why I'm here. I was fooling myself. But it's clear now."

"I went to church this morning. I haven't been there in years, except for Johnny's funeral," she said.

"For what?"

"For the way I feel with you. For pretending to be someone I'm not."

"Did you see *The Summer of Forty-Two? Harold and Maude?* It's nothing new, you and me."

"I raised you, Frank! This is not a movie. It's the real thing."

"Where do you think they get movies from?"

"Not *my* life."

"No, of course not yours."

Tears welled up in her eyes; she felt old.

"I'm sorry. Okay? Let's get out of here and get something to eat before my mother comes home," he said.

"I'm not hungry."

"*I am.*"

"There's left over turkey in the refrigerator. Zi'Aldo brought it over this morning."

"That's not the point. All right. I'll go," he said, annoyed. "The ball's in your court now, Lellie."

He let himself out. On the way home, he stopped at Nathan's in Coney Island where he double parked and bought himself two hot dogs and a large bag of greasy french fries that he ate in the car.

The next day was Saturday; Lella knew Frankie would be waiting for her. She went to her drawer and removed the only momento of Johnny's she had secretly salvaged from Carla's mad liquidation — a white linen handkerchief. She had washed that handkerchief, sprayed it with starch and ironed it many times. She had loved to launder Johnny's underwear. Before she put them into the wash, she would hold t-shirts up to her nose and take in Johnny's odor.

She caressed the cloth no longer warmed by its nearness to Johnny's body. She breathed in. It smelled more from perfumed articles of her own clothing that it had shared the drawer with than Johnny's scent. She realized that she didn't think about Johnny as much as she used to since she had begun spending time with his son.

She phoned Frankie. When he answered, she couldn't speak. She heard the Moody Blues blasting on the stereo: "Nights in white satin . . ." She hung up.

14

ICE CREAM AND DANDELIONS

Lella didn't see or talk to Frankie for almost a month. He met Carla for lunch in the city once or twice a week. Lella was jealous.

She phoned Frankie at work, and asked him to meet him at his apartment after work. When he got home, she was waiting at the door. She wore a camel wrap coat with a green and red plaid scarf draped loosely around her neck. Her hair was cut shorter than usual with wisps of it feathered around her face. She hadn't been there long; her nose was still red form the cold.

"New?" Frankie eyed her outfit.

"I got it at Lord and Taylor's. I used to go in just to ride the elevators."

"Nice getting a salary, isn't it?"

"Johnny always paid me."

"I mean a *real* salary." He tried to mask his nervousness with annoyance and sarcasm. "So how *is* your job?" He held the heavy steel door open for her.

"I like being with people."

"What do you know. Can I get you something?"

"I'll put a pot of coffee on," she said.

"No! I will."

"On second thought. I'd rather have tea."

"Don't you think I can make coffee?"

"I want tea," she said.

She sat on the couch and slid her coat off of her shoulders: nervous, she let it lie crumpled up behind her.

"Dolores is coming for Christmas," she said.

"I know. I'm picking her up at the airport." He filled a saucepan with water and set it on the stove.

"Any good movies playing?"

"Is that what you came here to ask me? You could have looked in the newspaper."

"I've missed you, Frank."

"Kills you to say it." He sat down beside her.

"This is a crazy situation," she said.

"Doesn't have to be."

She wanted him to make the first move this time, but she understood the DiGiacomo male stubborness. He had come to her once. It was her turn. She reached over and touched the knot of his tie and pulled him towards her.

He wrapped his arms around her and kissed her. He moved his hand down to the black knit dress and gently felt her breasts. Soon his hands were everywhere as he slid them under her dress, into her panties, messaging the fleshy buttocks. He undid her back zipper while she removed his jacket and began to unbutton his shirt. With his tie still knotted, her hands wandered inside and rubbed the hair on his chest.

"Let's go into the bedroom," he whispered.

She shook her head, afraid that if they stopped, even for a moment, it would all abruptly come to a halt. He undid her new black lace bra, pulling it down along with the dress. As he kissed her, he circled his fingers around her nipples until they stood up hard; then, while she held his head and kissed it all over, he buried his face into the life sustaining part of her body and sucked at the nipples until she thought he might actually get milk.

After his tongue had made its way down between her legs, after he had climbed on top of her and found his way in, after all that was left of the hot water was a burnt pot, she wondered if it ever dawned on him that she had done this before.

On Saturday morning Frankie drove Lella and Aldo up to the farm. Lella hadn't seen the old man so excited in years. He had long given up his license and no one had brought him up since Johnny and Louie's accident. They exited the Taconic Parkway and were about to turn onto the stony street when Aldo told Frankie to go a little further down the road. He directed him into the parking lot of an A&P.

"Stay here, I come right back."

Ten minutes later, they sat with their coats on in the cold kitchen: Aldo said it didn't pay to turn the heat on for such a short time. Aldo removed two jelly glasses and filled them with the vanilla ice cream and cream soda he had just bought. Grinning, he handed Frankie a glass overflowing with the frothy mixture.

"Just like ven you vas a boy und you und me come up here on the vinter veekends. You remember?" he said to Frankie.

"I remember."

Frankie took a sip and shivered.

When they finished, they took a tour of the grounds. Several inches of snow covered the fields and roof tops of the house and shed. Frankie dusted off a spot on the long white pole that had once served as a parking lot marker. There, Frankie made his proposal. He wanted to move up to the farm and take care of it. He wanted to have it long after Aldo and Regina were gone. He wanted to save it from falling into the hands of developers. This is where he wanted to be.

Aldo's head hung down while Frankie spoke. Lella gave Frankie an encouraging look.

"I don't sell," Aldo said.

"I don't want to buy it. I want to pay you rent. I'll bring you up here for the entire summer, or whenever you want."

"I don't vant no rent."

"Are you saying, no?"

"You have to promise me, someting, Francesco. Ven you grandmother und me die, dey vill vant to sell — Tony, Rose, you sister, Louie's boy. Dey vill all vant to sell. Den you buy."

"But what if they can get more than Frankie can offer?" Lella said.

"He voik hard und make sure he can! Und maybe I leave him a little help." Aldo winked. "Now I don't vorry about dis place no more. But I vorry about someting else."

Lella braced herself. He knew about them.

"Vat about school?" Aldo asked Frankie.

"I'm not cut out for numbers. I can't be an accountant like Uncle Tony. I'd like to be a counselor. Maybe in schools. Help kids. I can live here and go to the state college."

Frankie hadn't ever mentioned that part to Lella.

"Ven?"

"September."

"Vee settle a lot of business here today," Aldo said, putting one arm around Frankie and the other around Lella. "Und now vee go before you grandmother give our supper to dogs."

They walked towards the car, but Aldo veered away towards a patch of green grass where the sun had begun to melt the snow. Aldo knelt down on one knee. Leaning against the car, Frankie and Lella watched as Aldo took out his old rusty jackknife from his pants pocket and poked it several times into the ground

"This summer they be plenty *cicoria* here," he said.

There were no dogs. It was an expression Lella had heard Regina threaten Aldo with when he'd come home late from work. Supper was on the table when they arrived at Regina's: *cabbotzelle* — split goat's heads prepared with herbs and wine. Aldo's favorite. Regina quickly cleaned the *cicoria* Aldo had picked up for her at the corner vegetable stand on his way home, and she added some to the salad: the rest she would saute in garlic and oil for tomorrow's lunch. After supper she brought out four fresh peaches, refusing to reveal how she had gotten hold of them this time of year. With strong or with feeble hands, they sliced the peaches and stuffed them

into their wine glasses, letting the dark liquid soak into
the sugary fruit, until the yellow peaches took on a
purplish cast, and the sweetness and tartness comple-
mented one another.

15

FRANKIE KISSES LELLA

"Where are we going to put three babies in this apartment?" Carla lit a cigarette.

"We'll make room," Lella said. "Just five days. The children can sleep in my room, Dolores and Scott in Frank's old room, and I'll sleep with you."

Carla scowled.

"Five days, Carla." Lella opened the large carton that held the Christmas ornaments and stared at the naked tree in the living room.

"I haven't had babies in this house for so long, I don't know what they need," Carla said.

"You didn't know when you had them."

"I managed fine with Dolores before you came."

"What did Dolores say to get?"

"Huggies diapers — not Pampers, mind you — the purple box. Apple juice. Baldies."

"Baldies?"

"Hard pretzels without salt. The younger one is cutting a tooth. And get rid of the candy, she said."

"Why?"

"She doesn't allow it. *Compare* Dominick's daughter didn't let *her* daughter eat candy and she started stealing it at the supermarket. Now she's sixteen and she steals nail polish and hair spray."

"What are their names again?" Lella asked.

"Phoebe, Lisa, and Cory — or Lori. Something like that."

"Waspy names."

"Dolores didn't name them. Should they call me Grandma?"

"Of course. What about me?"

"Lella. That's your name, isn't it?"

"Maybe they should call me Aunt or Cousin."

"How about Your Highness?"

"Go to hell."

"I don't know why we're putting up a tree," Carla put out her cigarette.

Lella wasn't sure if Carla meant it was too soon after Johnny's death, or if she just didn't want to be bothered."

"For the children," Lella said.

"It doesn't feel like Christmas, Lellie."

Lella sighed.

"No," she said.

☆

Carla decided the baby's disposable diapers would be wrapped in old newspaper and immediately brought down to the garbage pails in the alley. She was amazed how capably Dolores managed the children. Cory, the youngest child, not quite two, took a liking to Carla.

Whenever Carla sat in her overstuffed chair, the little girl climbed into her lap, thumb in mouth, fingers twisting a lock of hair. Carla made cookies with the children and, to the family's amazement, got down on the rug and played Candy Land with them. After three days, she was exhausted and relieved that everyone but herself was going over to the DiGiacomo's for Christmas Eve dinner.

On Christmas morning Dolores's family gathered around the tree that Carla and Lella had decorated. Lella felt uncomfortable. The room was small and wherever she seemed to be, so was Frankie, brushing up against her arm, inadvertently touching her hand, as they all chaotically handed gifts to one another. It was a challenge to be together around the family: wanting to be near him, trying to be inconspicuous. Lella avoided Frankie's eyes, but she felt him watching her, following her every move. Because of her preoccupation with Frankie, Lella failed to notice yet another family member who was observing her.

While the children opened presents and Frankie thought no one was looking, he caught Lella's attention and motioned for her to leave the room. Suddenly they were gone.

Dolores found them in Lella's bedroom.

"I wanted to wish you a Merry Christmas," Frankie whispered, standing face to face with Lella.

From the doorway, Dolores watched him kiss Lella long and hard on the mouth.

After breakfast, Dolores invited Frankie and Lella for a walk, but Frankie protested it was too cold.

"Colder than Alaska?" she wanted to know.

When they reached the corner, she opened fire on them:

"What the hell is going on?"

"What do you mean?" Frankie said.

"I saw the two of you," Dolores said.

They walked down the avenue with determination; he, staring down at the pavement, Lella and Dolores straight ahead.

"We're in love," Frankie said.

"Are you crazy?" Dolores shouted.

"Lower it, Dolores," Frankie said.

"Nobody's around. They're all inside eating." She turned to Lella. "Why? You're almost our mother."

"For a long time I wanted to be your mother," Lella said.

"She's *not* our mother. *You* always thought of her as a mother. I never did. I already had a mother," Frankie said.

They entered the park and sat down on an empty set of swings. Dolores kicked the cement ground with her heels. She restlessly turned from side to side, twisting the seat and its chains.

"I assume Mom doesn't know," Dolores said.

"Mom's only concerned with herself," Frankie said.

"So now you're punishing her for not paying attention to you? You can't get comfort from one mother, so you try another. How convenient to have two mothers!"

"You're being unfair, Dolores." Lella got up and faced Dolores.

"Are you afraid you won't have Lella to yourself anymore? Or are you afraid this won't cut your husband's waspy standards?" Frankie said.

"You're sick!" Dolores told Frankie.

"Maybe the situation we were brought up in was a little sick," Frankie said.

"That's enough!" Lella cried.

"Don't reprimand us. We're not children anymore," Dolores said.

"Then stop acting like it," Lella said.

"I always thought you were the mature one," Dolores told Frankie.

"I didn't go looking for this," Frankie said.

"Like hell."

"It's true," Lella confirmed.

"Lella is what I need right now," Frankie said.

"Well you can't have her! She's just filling some gap," Dolores said.

"Scott needed a mother for his kids. You filled one hell of a gap for him," Frankie said.

"That had nothing to do with us being together."

"Everything has something to do with everything. That's how relationships form. Cause and effect. That's life," Frankie said.

"What could you two possibly have in common?"

"A lifetime," Lella answered.

Dolores stopped moving around. She grew quiet.

"I used to think that maybe you were my real mother," Dolores said to Lella.

"Why?" Lella asked alarmed.

"I don't know. I guess I just really wanted you to be my mother."

"I'm moving up to the farm in March," Frankie changed the subject.

"Why would you want to be there?"

"I love that place, Dolores. I always have."

"You too?" Dolores asked Lella.

"We haven't discussed it," she said.

"Don't wait to tell Mom. Don't make a fool out of her," Dolores told them.

"Why are *you* so protective of her all of a sudden?" Frank asked.

"She's right, Frank," Lella said.

"Things are different. She's respects me more now that I'm married and have the kids," Dolores said.

"Maybe you're different too," Lella said.

"When I first walked into the apartment, it hit me that Dad was never coming back. Remember when we were kids and we'd have a great day at the farm. Frank would ask how many more days were left of vacation. Then he'd say, 'We have five more days or three more days of today.' I wish we could have one more day of yesterday. Just one," Dolores said.

"When I woke up this morning, I smelled garlic and onions frying. For a minute I thought nothing had changed. I'd go into the kitchen and dunk toast in coffee and Dad would walk in, clean shaven, grinning," Frankie said.

"Then he'd rub his hands together and say, 'Smells good!' " Dolores added.

The three smiled.

"You think you'll ever move back? I miss you," Frankie told Dolores.

"I miss you too. But I'm not like you, Frank. I don't need to be here," she said, looking up at Lella.

☆

Two days after Dolores left, Carla was back in the hospital. Carla's doctor was out of town, and the covering physician read her medical history and listened to her complaints. He observed an enlarged spleen, swollen ankles, and skin eruptions over the bridge of her nose. He called in a rheumatologist who ordered a battery of tests. Several days later, the doctor's suspicions were confirmed: the swelling and fatigue were due to kidney failure; the kidney failure was due to a greater influencing ailment that had been inhabiting Carla's body for years. The achy joints and bronchial problems were all the result of a disease that defied diagnosis, a malady not uncommonly labeled hypochondria, a blood disease called Lupus. She was placed on steroids and would be monitored frequently. There was no cure. Maybe as soon as five years from now, she might become liable to a fatal bacteria, or succumb to heart failure, or hemorrhage to death.

Lella came home at noon to fix Carla's lunch. She took her on short walks, and administered her medicine until Carla felt well enough to return to work. One evening at the kitchen table, Frankie and Lella told Carla about their affair Carla sat quietly for awhile, as though processing the information. Lella and Frankie waited.

"Is this the toy salesman? Or are you on a roll?"

Then Carla features knitted tightly together and she spat out her words like the old Italian women spat saliva at one another to show their disgust.

"I took you into my home, treated you like my *comare*, and you repay me first by throwing yourself all over my husband and now my son."

"Ma! Stop it!" Frankie cried.

"There was nothing between me and Johnny," Lella said. And I never meant for Frankie and me . . ."

"But you never did anything to avoid it!"

"That's not true!" Lella insisted.

"Did you leave when we told you to go? Did you start your own life? No. You fed on mine. You dug deeper and deeper until you were so attached, God Almighty couldn't have dragged you away," Carla shouted.

"You wanted me, Carla. So you could have your freedom, be a modern woman. You slept with Johnny every night, not me!"

"It wasn't enough you wanted to be my son's mother. You had to be his lover too! *Puttana!*" Whore, she called Lella, as she went over to the china cabinet drawer. "God robbed me of my husband, but I won't watch you take my son," she grumbled as she took a letter from the drawer and threw it on the table for Frankie and Lella to read:

January 10th, 1975
Dear Mom,

When Frankie told me about your illness, I became distraught. Not being able to see you right away put all sorts of crazy notions in my head about your state and regrets in my heart about our relationship. If I could just visit you in person, it would let me cope with this much better. But I can't leave the children just now.

Are you frightened? That bothers me most. Are you at peace with yourself should anything happen suddenly? Mom, these are questions I could never ask you, and I don't write them to scare you. Only because I love you and am concerned with how you are dealing with this new blow.

I've been thinking that it would really be wonderful for you to get away — not for just a week or two, but for good. You've never been out of Brooklyn! Wouldn't you like to try someplace new?

New scenery, new climate, new people?

There's a new complex of condominiums several blocks from our home. There are still several condos available and I was thinking how nice it would be to have you close. There would be a swimming pool, sauna, and lemon trees right in your backyard. We could see one another more often, without the tension of every visit having to be such a big ordeal, and you could help me with the children. They really like you.

We've never had that kind of time together in our family, Mom, just you and me. You understand what I'm saying.

Scott is very excited about your moving to Phoenix. Many of our friends' parents are retiring here. You would have plenty of new friends.

Please think about this and let us know. I am enclosing a brochure on the condominiums. I like the two-bedroom! I'll call soon. Please say yes.

Love,
Dolores

"I didn't understand it at first, but now it's clear. Dolores knows, doesn't she? And I always doubted my daughter's love. What fools we can be," Carla said.

Lella turned to the brochure; Carla grabbed it out of her hands. That's my world, all mine, her actions said.

Carla put her house up for sale; she planned to give notice at work.

16

CARLA DANCES THE TARANTELLA

Spring arrived early in New York, and Frankie wasted no time in moving up to the farm. He wanted Aldo and Regina to be comfortable in the Big House which he and Lella had come to realize was not a big house at all, but a very small one. They had all managed to fit in it and make it seem grand, or had it always been insufferably small to adults and only large from a child's view? Perhaps their needs had been fewer then and their hearts bigger.

Frankie asked Lella to move into the bungalow with him when it was finished, but she refused to make a commitment. They had not even told Aldo and Regina about their relationship: now he wanted them to *live* together as a couple. And then there was Carla. She had not gotten a buyer for the house and, therefore, still hadn't told her boss she was leaving.

Although the women moved about in silence, Lella watched out for Carla, making sure the refrigerator was stocked, Carla's medicine refilled, even Carla's clothes laundered. At times, Lella sensed that Carla wanted to make up and get on with their lives. Lella would ask Carla what she desired for dinner, or what she wanted to watch on television, and Carla would begin to casually answer her, but then she caught herself and resumed silence. Lella kept hoping that one morning Carla would gather up the whole situation in a dustpan and dump it into the trash, put it behind them. That's the way it always used to happen: Carla got her agression out; things went on just as before. But this time Carla wouldn't budge, and Lella knew she had trespassed on most sacred territory.

On Palm Sunday morning an article in *The New York Times* caught Lella's eye: preparations for the pipeline had begun. Eight major oil companies had formed the Alyeska Pipeline Service and were building the three hundred and sixty mile road from the Yukon River to Prudhoe Bay. She cut the article out, put it into her purse, and went over to Aldo and Regina's where she found Aldo and Frankie sitting at the kitchen table, whittling stalks of palm that Rose's children had brought back from Church. With penknives, they made miniature baskets and crosses to be worn on lapels. Regina was cooking at the extra stove in the basement.

"Have you heard about the pipeline?" Lella took a seat next to Frankie and whispered so that Aldo couldn't hear.

He nodded, concentrating on the palm.

"Are you going?"

"Depends. I've made some promises to Nonno. To finish school for one. He's counting on me to look after them and the farm for awhile. And it depends on you. Have you decided yet?"

"I can't tell them." She indicated Aldo.

"Nonno!" Frankie called loudly.

Aldo looked up from his work.

"I'm in love with Lella, Nonno."

"Frank!" Lella shrieked.

The old man put down his penknife and palm and picked up his pipe. He stirred the tobacco in the pipe with the corner of an open matchbook. Then he held a lighted match over the tobacco and drew on it until the shreds of tobacco glowed. He took the pipe out of his mouth and let an aromatic puff fill the air. He stared at them, his eyes squinting with confusion.

"Vhat?"

"Lella and me. We're in love."

Aldo looked to Lella. Her expression told him it was true. "If our agreement is off, I understand, Nonno," Frankie said.

Aldo took another draw from his pipe; his lips broke into a faint smile of surprise.

"Sometimes vee have to close our eyes or vee lose it all."

Puzzled, Lella looked to Frankie. He shrugged his shoulders.

"*È il destino*. I don' fight mit destiny."

"We'll get over it," Lella offered apologetically.

"What do you mean?" Frankie cried.

Aldo looked at Lella with tired blue eyes — Johnny's eyes — and in Italian he told her not to make a lie out of love.

It was Holy Saturday, and Lella helped Regina bake Easter pies. While Aldo sat on the porch, smoking a pipe, the women took a coffee break.

"Papa," Carla surprised Aldo with her greeting and walked past him. In her high heels she stomped through the parlor and dining room, the floor vibrating and the stemware in the china cabinet rattling with each step. She found Lella and Regina in the kitchen: Regina in her starched housedress, white anklets, and black orthopedic shoes; Lella in a t-shirt and jeans. Regina was so surprised to see Carla, she dropped the hard biscuit she had been dunking into her coffee, and the coffee spilled out over the cup. Lella jumped up, grabbed a wet dish towel, and sponged the black liquid that was spreading into the white linen tablecloth.

"*Lascialo sta'.*" Regina held her hand out in front of Lella like a policeman stopping traffic and ordered her to let the cleaning go. A matter of greater importance had presented itself.

"Sit, Carla." Regina gestured with her hand.

"No! I'll stand as long as I like. I'll do whatever I please in this house. For twenty-seven years I've done what you wanted, you the Queen Mother who smoked and starved herself, ruled her sons, and did anything she could think of to get attention — "

"Carla!" Lella interrupted.

"She's mad," Regina whispered to Lella.

"I'm mad all right. How do you think people get crazy? They're driven to it by selfish women like yourselves. Women who only get pleasure by taking from others. You wanted me to talk to you, Lella. I'm talking . . . so now you talk." Having purged herself, Carla seemed at a loss for anything more to say.

"Look, Carla, I never planned this, but you and Johnny were right when you said I was entitled to my own happiness."

"Well, I didn't raise a son for your happiness."

"It hasn't only been Frankie that's made me happy. My life would be nothing without all of you. You were — and are my life."

"I can't forgive you," Carla said solemnly.

"Then why are you here, Carla?" Lella asked.

"Because I'm losing my life."

"Eh, who isn't?" Regina murmured.

"I'm tired, Lella, I'm so tired of being angry. And I miss my son."

Lella nervously got up and carried the cups, which shook in her hands, over to the sink.

"You lost Johnny, Carla. The rest of us are still here," Lella said.

Regina began to tap her fingers on the table. She began humming. "Stop it!" Carla ordered, but Regina continued humming, staring straight at Carla.

"I'm sorry, Carla. I am. But it's not the worst thing. Sometimes it almost makes sense. Think about it."

"I have been thinking," Carla said. "And it makes no sense to me at all. You don't know how hard this has been."

Lella looked down. How could this ever be right? How could they ever make it better?

"Maybe it's my fault. When I brought you into our home, I gave up control over my children. I gave up my children," Carla said.

"No, Carla. You're children love you. *You're* their mother. And you are who you are. Give in, Carla."

Regina pushed back the metal-framed chair and took small steps towards the center of the room. As she hummed, she motioned to Lella to join her.

"You're crazy!" Carla said.

"Remember *compare* Dominick's daughter's wedding?" Lella said to Carla. Remember how no one wanted to start the tarantella, but you and I did — alone? Before we knew it two hundred people got up. It was total chaos. The floor was shaking so much the maître d' got scared and called the fire department. Remember?" Lella said.

Lella could tell Carla was trying not to smile.

"Carla," Regina called. "You always like a'the tarantella. You always tell a'the music man to play it, but I tell a'you, 'Sit down. Stay quiet. You make *una brutta figura*. You make us all look a'bad.' You remember?"

"You're damn right I remember."

"Come, Carla. I give a'you you Tarantella."

"Drop dead."

"Soon."

"You promise?"

"*Ma* sure. First you dance."

"God forgive you, Carla," Lella said. Then she burst out laughing.

Lella reached out for Carla.

"What do you think this is? A scene from *The Most Happy Fella'* or something?" Carla said.

Lella knew she and Regina looked comical together because, against her will, Carla began to laugh. Reluctantly, Carla joined hands with Lella.

"You never did it right. Let me show you," Carla said.

They circled to the right, to the left, Lella humming the melody; Carla joining in. High, they held their hands up and moved towards each other, standing so close to one another Lella could feel Carla's hip bones. Regina stood apart from them, tapping out the beat with her heavy black foot. Faster and faster Carla and Lella spun, as though they were suspended in life, dangling from nothing more than the threads of their passions.

"*Ma questa è una casa di pazzi!*" Aldo announced as he stood in the doorway of the kitchen. "Yes." He shook his head. "Dis a crazy house for sure."

☆

That night, Carla went to bed without taking Vallium. The ringing of the phone at eleven-twenty did not wake her. It was Lella who picked up the receiver.

"I tried to get Mom earlier, but nobody was home."

"We were at your grandmother's," Lella said.

"*Mom* was at Nonna's?"

"We both were."

"I have to tell her something."

"Is everyone all right, Dolores?"

"We're fine. It's about the move."

"You changed your mind?"

"No. Scott received orders to go to Germany for two years. There's a new training program being put into operation and he has to go. We leave in a few months. I hate to tell Mom."

"You know what they say: The best laid plans . . .""

"She can still come. We could settle her in. Then we'll be back."

"It's a good thing she hasn't sold the house yet, or quit her job. Can she get back the deposit on the condo?"

"Yes. Don't worry about the deposit."

"It just wasn't meant to be," Lella said.

"It's easy for you to say that it wasn't meant to be, Lellie."

"Dolores. Your mother will never be alone. I promise."

"It was a great idea! And we'll do it when we get back."

"Of course."

"How is she doing?"

"Good. Today was a good day. Do you want me to tell Carla?"

"No. I'll call her tomorrow."

"Don't worry about it, Dolores. Your mother is a strong lady."

"One more thing, Lellie. I'm pregnant."

"Oh, Dolores! *Four* children?"

"Please don't start, Lellie. You sound like my mother."

"Take care of yourself, Dolores. Take care of that baby."

"I will. Goodnight."

Lella sensed that Carla would be relieved. Hadn't Carla really only been running away from Lella and

Frankie? But now Carla and she had reconnected, and tomorrow Carla would make her peace with Frankie. Besides, Lella was finally realizing that, despite Carla's talk and appearing to be different from the rest of them, she was a woman fearful of change and terribly insecure.

17

LELLA BRINGS CARLA TO THE COUNTRY

On a Saturday morning in June, Carla and Lella drove up to the farm for the day. The bungalow was finished. In a week, Aldo and Regina would be arriving, and Lella wanted to have everything in the big house clean and in place for them.

"Your father would be proud. But it could use shutters." Carla studied the white shingled bungalow with its open green porch.

"What color would you like?" Frankie asked.

"What does it matter what I like?"

"I won't beat around the bush, Mom. I want you to come up and live here in the bungalow."

"You and me in that small bungalow?"

"No. Just you. We can stay in the big House until I build another one. There's enough room here for ten bungalows."

"We?"

"I'm moving up here too," Lella said.

"Why didn't you tell me?"

"I wanted to be sure. I got a job in a nursing home. Will you come, Carla?"

"What would I do here?"

"What were you going to do in Phoenix?" Frankie asked.

"I was going to make friends."

"There are people here too," Lella said.

"But they're far. I can't even drive."

"I'll teach you," Frankie said.

"It's probably better things didn't materialize with Dolores. I really don't want to stop working. I'm afraid if I stop, my life might stop with it. Can you two understand? I have to keep going; I have to keep up my pace. Besides, Frankie, I really couldn't live here all summer with your grandmother!"

"There's a lot of space between the Big House and the bungalow. You'd have plenty of privacy. You could even find a job here."

She took in the distance from the cottage to the house. It was substantial, but she said, no.

"When's the wedding?" Carla asked.

"We want to be together first for awhile — try our relationship on for size," Frankie said.

"How trendy," Carla said.

"This all still bothers you, doesn't it?" Frankie put his arm around his mother.

"Why don't you move up here," Lella said. She felt terribly guilty about leaving Carla. Moreover, she was frightened; part of Lella couldn't imagine herself without Carla.

"Don't worry about me. When it gets bad, I'll let you know. I can come up on weekends. Spend my vacation here. *Try it on for size*. But I belong in the house in Bensonhurst. It's my home."

"Summer came so early. Just like spring did. Everything's moving so fast. Everything's changing," Carla told Lella on the ride back to Bensonhurst.

At home, Carla couldn't sleep. It was eleven o'clock and still eighty degrees. She went downstairs and sat on the shiny red steps. Lella joined her.

Old lady Yahtzbin was perched on her own side, her bony legs, spread wide apart, extended out from a thin cotton shift. She was smoking a cigarette. When she saw Carla and Lella, she got up and slowly went over to them. She parked herself between Carla and one of the stone lions and offered Carla a Marlboro.

"You know I'm not supposed to smoke. Why do you? I thought you were a health nut."

"Because I am like you, Mrs. Johnny. I am hypocrite. Look at me. Ninety-one years and it does not hurt me one bit."

"Your breath stinks and your teeth are brown."

"Like yours, Mrs. Johnny. You are like me."

"There's something I've always wanted to tell you, Mrs. Yahtzbin. Go to hell."

"You are dirty tongued, Mrs. Johnny."

"Like you, Mrs. Yahtzbin."

"You think you are better than me, don't you?"

"I'm different, thank God."

"You are not different. Both of you. You are like me. You are alone. Abandoned. Left to die. Like dogs you vill die alone — like me."

"I have two things to tell you, Mrs. Yahtzbin," Lella said. "Move onto your own side of the stoop and blow your smoke in the opposite direction of us. I have one more thing to say: *you* may be alone, but *we* are not."

The old woman cursed, got up, and went back to her side of the stoop.

A man appeared; he was carrying two pails full of coal towards the alley. He looked at Lella, winked and smiled, then he said to Mrs. Yahtzbin, "There's no need to talk to my wife like that, young lady." Then he disappeared.

"Carla, I never saw you cry after Johnny died. Why?"

"Frankie asked me that recently."

"And?"

"I was angry at Johnny because I never got the chance to tell him how unhappy I was all those years."

"But what were you unhappy about?"

"Him, his family. And everything about me! You know I was conceived on the ship my parents took when they left Sicily and came here."

"So?"

"My spirit got left somewhere in the ocean, trying to decide which way to go. I wanted to be different, but I couldn't! Even you were able to change. Isn't that something? You got free, but I couldn't!"

"But why blame Johnny?"

"Because! I thought he was different. I thought we would change together."

"What did Frankie say to all that?" Lella asked.

"Not to blame Johnny for what I never did, and not to punish you and him because my parents made love on a boat."

"Sounds like Johnny," Lella said.

"I never saw much of Johnny in Frankie until today. Even though Frankie's eyes are brown, they're dove-shaped like Johnny's. Have you noticed? His chin, it's not really pointed like mine, but squarish like Johnny's. Frankie is broad like Johnny. And he's kind like Johnny."

Carla began to shiver.

"What is it?" Lella asked.

Carla shook her head, but Lella knew that Carla was in pain; that she ached so bad; she ached for Johnny.

Lella placed her hand over Carla's to comfort her: Carla had lost Johnny, but Lella had Frankie.

ACKNOWLEDGMENTS

I am grateful to Antonio D'Alfonso, Joseph Nocera, Julie Rose, Jeane Schinto, Tom Marantz, and to the Lyman Road writers: Joann Kobin, Mordicai Gerstein, Norman Kotker, Betsy Hartmann, John Stifler, and especially Anthony Giardina for his inexhaustible patience and advice. And to my husband, Marty Wohl, who makes all things possible, to Ariana, Carina, and Michael, and to Marcelo Fernandez who first encouraged me to write.

Printed in March 1999 by

in Longueuil, Quebec